# ICED

## DEFIANT KINGS
### BOOK THREE

## BELLA MATTHEWS

# SENSITIVE CONTENT

This book contains sensitive content that could be triggering.

Please see my website for a full list.

WWW.AUTHORBELLAMATTHEWS.COM

Editor: Dena Mastrogiovanni, Red Pen Editing

Cover Designer: Shannon Passmore, Shanoff Designs

Photographer: Jane Ashley Converse, J Ashley Converse Photography

Cover Models: Maddi Hansen & Dane Peterson

Interior Formatting: Brianna Cooper

*To strong women.*
*May we know them.*
*May we raise them.*
*May we be them.*

*This book is dedicated to my niece, Alex, the original Dr. Esher, who is one of the strongest women I know. Thank you for always answering every single crazy medical question I have and never laughing at me for my excitement over new ways to torture and kill my characters.*

"I am the master of my fate, I am the captain of my soul."

— WILLIAM ERNEST HENLEY

.

# PROLOGUE

## INDIA

*February . . .*

"Remind me again why I'm torturing myself?" I don't bother hiding my sarcasm from my brother. Sarcasm is our love language. It's been that way since we were little. Besides, something tells me he can hear my eye roll through the other end of the call and he's smiling.

Atlas is always smiling.

"I swear, it's raining. We're short-staffed at The Bee today, and I'm already late. I should just go home and help Gramps." I leave off that, thanks to an unfortunately placed puddle in the parking lot, my ballet flats are soaked, and I may or may not have stabbed my eyeball trying to put on mascara while I was driving here this morning.

Well . . . not while actually driving. More like stopped at a red light.

Not my proudest moment. But in my defense, my lashes are blonde, and not dark-blonde either. They're pale as hell. It's not a good look. Something that was pointed out to me on a daily basis in high school before my mom finally gave in and let me wear makeup.

Teenage girls are assholes, by the way.

"Breathe, Indy. Your version of late is what the rest of us call early. I know Gramps says on time is late, and five minutes early is on time, but it's really not."

I swear Atlas was blessed with all the laid-back genes when he was born. They skipped over me completely and double-dosed him eleven months later. "I'm breathing, smart-ass. I just really want this job. I only have a few months before my student loans kick in."

Atlas groans as I hurry to a stop in front of the school. "You could always defer them."

"Yeah, I know. But the interest rate for that is sky-high, and I don't want to set myself up to be poor for the rest of my life." Spending the past two decades that way has been more than enough to last a lifetime.

I look around for the buzzer most elementary schools have outside the office doors, then smile when I find it in exactly the same place it seems to be at every school where I've interviewed in the past six months. "Listen, I'm about to walk in. I've got to go. Wish me luck." I end the call before he answers and force my shoulders back before I push the button.

This one will be the one.

I can feel it.

This will be the school that hires me.

~

Two hours later, I'm rethinking every decision I've made over the past four years. Each one carefully deliberated and meticulously planned out. The only one that technically worked out was graduating from college in three and a half years instead of four. One less semester's worth of student loans means less to pay back. It's the whole getting-a-job-after-graduation that seems to be blowing up in my face.

"Slow down, Indy. What did they say?" My friend Sophie hands me a salted caramel latte from across the bakery counter at Sweet Temptations and boxes up a few desserts for me while she listens to me bitch about another failed interview. Well, more like for me to take across the street to the café my grandfather owns.

"He didn't say anything," I somehow manage to hold back the tears threatening to spill. "That's the problem. It was another blow off. Nobody wants to hire a kindergarten teacher with no experience. But how can I get experience without having the job?" I throw my hands in the air. Angry. Sad. Frustrated. The whole myriad of emotions battling with each other. "I give up."

The bells chime over the door before I have a chance to thank her, and the shop owner's cousin-in-law waltzes in like he owns the place.

Dark suit.

Darker hair.

And the darkest brown eyes locked on Sophie with a laser focus which gives me chills.

"How are we doing today, ladies?" Dean DeLaurentis strolls to the counter for his daily dose of flirting with my friend. I take that as my cue to pick up my boxes and coffee and get the hell out of here.

The man is sex-on-a-stick hot, but he's a little scary. And he knows it. And I stay as far away from scary as I can. I've had enough scary to last a lifetime.

"Thanks again, Sophie. See you later." I stop once I'm outside but still under the awning of the building and carefully balance my coffee on the boxes with one hand so I can pull my hood over my head, since apparently the rain has picked back up.

But while I'm wrangling with my hood, a sleek black sports car comes to a screeching halt at the curb in front of me. The momentum sprays muddy puddle water all over me, and I cringe.

Some days, you should stay in bed.

Go with your gut and go back to sleep instead of adulting.

Today is one of those days.

"Shit," a deep voice says before a car door slams shut. "I didn't see you there."

"Yeah . . . Apparently." I shake out my wet hand before grabbing my coffee from the top of the boxes and looking up. *And up.* Umm . . . and up.

*Damn.*

This man is tall. Well over six feet with shoulders I'm pretty sure wouldn't fit through a door frame without turning sideways. I'm guessing he's an athlete. *A hot athlete.* One who's probably got big hands to go with that big body. I wonder what else is big.

"Shit. I made you wet."

"Excuse me?" I step back, my unsteady boxes already forgotten.

"The puddle," he answers, and I say a quick mental thank-you that I hadn't accidently verbalized anything about his . . . umm . . . size. Big hands—*yup, knew they'd be big*—reach out to help me keep hold of the damn desserts before they crash to the ground. "What did you think I meant?" he asks with a cocky, knowing tone.

Warm goosebumps dance over my skin in a way that hasn't happened in years—*freaking years*—until I shut that down. I refuse to indulge in that line of thinking. This guy screams bad news. Probably not for everyone . . . but definitely for me.

I don't do bad news anymore.

Been there. Done that. Got the consolation prize to show for it.

Shit. What was the question?

He bends his knees, bringing himself down a few inches to my eye level.

No surprise, his eyes are as gorgeous as the rest of him.

"Hey. It's just a little water." He pulls me farther under the shop's canopy, and his brow furrows. "You're not gonna cry, are you?" Concern quickly replaces confusion. "Please don't cry. I suck with crying women."

"Do you make women cry often?" I ask. This man doesn't get to know I was ready to cry long before he splashed me.

"Hell no. I have four sisters, and three of them would join together to kick my ass if I made a girl cry." He laughs like it's the most natural thing in the world, and holy hell, that sound. It does things it has absolutely no business doing to me.

"Only three of your sisters? Is your fourth sister a secret sadist or something?" I taunt as I step away from him, tightening my hold on the pink boxes.

The big guy smiles, and I may actually melt. "No. My fourth sister came out of the sadist closet on her sixth birthday last year. We're all well aware of her mean tendencies now."

I bite down on my bottom lip, refusing to laugh. I've met this guy a million times. Not *this one* in particular but so many like him. This town is full of them. Rich, cocky, gorgeous college kids who've been given everything without having to work for it a single day in their lives. He looks pretty on the outside, but I'd bet he's about as deep as that puddle he splashed me with.

I look him over one more time because there's nothing that says I can't appreciate how gorgeous this one is before I shake my head free of my lusty thoughts and tuck them away for later.

"Do you have a name, pretty girl?"

"I sure do," I tell him before I dart across the street and back to my day from hell.

~

*J*ace

Well, that was interesting.

I thought I knew everyone in this town. At least, every *woman* . . . Okay, fine. I know the *hot* ones. And that woman—the one who just ran away from me like her cute little ass was on fire—is fucking gorgeous.

I stand in front of my sister's bakery, watching the petite blonde push through the door of The Busy Bee and hand someone her ridiculous stack of pink boxes before disappearing behind a door. *Looks like it's time for a little recon.*

"Hey, Sophie." I approach the counter and smile at Amelia's manager, who's completely immune to my charm.

The guy she's flirting with eyes me like a bug he'd like to squash with his shiny shoe but can't because his boss—the one who runs the whole damn city—happens to be my brother-in-law. And because I like pissing people off, I lean across the counter and wipe a little flour off Sophie's cheek.

"What are you doing here, Jace? Aren't you supposed to be in class?" she asks, fluttering her eyelashes from me to Dean. Then she scrunches her nose and stares at me. "Have you been drinking?"

"Nah. Maybe still hungover from yesterday though. You know how it is. Anyway, I wanted to stop in and see the prettiest baker in town before class." So maybe I'm laying it on a little thick, but I need a favor.

"Jesus Christ," Dean mutters under his breath. "I'm outta here, Sophie."

"Bye, Dean." She smiles all dreamy and shit as he walks away, then glares at me like one of my sisters would before she fills a cup of coffee and hands it over. "You know you're an asshole, Jace Kingston."

I chuckle and take the coffee before she can spit in it. "Whatever. That guy's an idiot for not asking you out already."

"Who says I'd say yes?" She opens a pink bag and tosses a blueberry muffin and a few napkins in it, then throws it at my chest. When I catch it but don't answer, she caves. "Fine. I'd say yes. Fuck it. I'd say let me have your babies. But he's not asking. So how about you tell me what has you so happy on a Friday morning?"

I met Sophie when she started working for my sister my senior year of high school. I've never had friends who are girls. That's because I'm pretty sure I couldn't be friends with a girl without wanting to fuck her. The thought's crossed my mind once or twice with Sophie, but my sister Amelia laid down the law years ago. No dating her employees. Ever.

Probably a good move.

"Who was the girl who left the shop before I walked in?"

She thinks about it for a minute, then lifts her hand midway up my chest. "About yay high, blonde hair, lots of pink boxes?"

"Yeah."

The little brat smiles and shakes her head. "I have no idea who you're talking about."

"Come on, Sophie. She just went into The Busy Bee. How have I never seen her before?" This is bugging the shit out of me.

"Guess you're oblivious, Kingston." The bells above the doors chime, and an older couple walks in. "Hi, Mr. and Mrs.

Walker." Sophie glances back at me. "Better get to class, Jace. Have a good game tonight."

I flip her off and grab my bag and coffee. "Payback's a bitch, Sophie."

~

*I* crack my eyes open the next morning when a warm body curls up against my side.

A body I don't remember going to bed with.

My head pounds a nasty rhythm, and my stomach revolts. Never a good way to wake up.

I inch away, but she throws her arm over my chest and purrs . . . like a fucking cat.

This is why I don't do sleepovers. I like my space. Not a clingy puck bunny who sees me as the ticket to her MRS degree. When I roll over and away from her, though, it's not to cool sheets and an empty pillow. Without opening my eyes, I groan, knowing a tight little ass just backed itself right up against my dick.

Two women.

Damn. Now I really wish I could remember last night.

The arm wrapped around my chest from behind begins moving down toward my boxers.

*Hey . . . I'm wearing boxers.*

That's either a very good thing or a very bad thing.

I chance it and force my eyes open, only to immediately slam them shut when my skull threatens to crack in half from the sudden invasion of light.

Oh, man . . .

This isn't normal.

What the hell did I do last night?

*Earlier tonight?*

Shit, I don't even know what day it is.

8

A little more carefully this time, I slowly peel open one eye and give my brain time to adjust to the bright light shining from my ceiling fan before attempting to open the other eye. The pounding in my head intensifies when I try to take stock of my surroundings before I get stuck on a familiar pile of messy jet-black hair in front of me. Hair covering a face I think I should know, but I'm pretty sure I'm either still too drunk or more massively hungover than ever before.

But this doesn't feel like a hangover. This isn't from booze and a little weed. *Trust me*, I've had plenty of nights like that, and I never wake up feeling like this.

*What the hell?*

I try to piece together what happened, but everything's a blur after we came home from the game and started drinking. I remember kicking Boston University's ass on the ice Friday afternoon. I remember coming back to the hockey house and tapping the keg. I think I remember beer pong. Then nothing . . .

I try to force myself to remember something, *anything*, but all my thoughts slowly scatter when the warm hand trailing up and down my abs pushes under the band of my boxers and wraps around my cock.

"Hey, Daddy," a woman purrs in my ear, and I inch away.

*Seriously?*

Do women think that voice is sexy? Even worse, what twenty-two-year-old wants to be called *Daddy*? Not this one. I've got enough daddy issues of my own to last two fucking lifetimes. I don't need a girl with one too.

I move to sit up when my bedroom door flies open and cracks against the wall. "What the fuck?" My roommate, Sean pushes through the crowd of people gathering in the hall.

My head spins when I sit up and look at his face. It's a

deep, pissed-off shade of purple that grows ten shades darker when he looks at the women on either side of me.

That's when I realize where I know that head of black hair from.

*Oh shit.*

She's his girlfriend.

I turn my head to look at cat-girl.

*Fuck me.*

"You fucked my girlfriend and my sister?" he shouts and I scramble out of bed, ducking the fist flying at my face without the movement actually cracking open my skull.

What the fuck did I drink last night?

"You're gonna die, Kingston."

Probably not the best time to tell him I was fucking her at the beginning of the season.

The girlfriend. Not the sister.

In my defense, it was before they started dating, and I was probably too drunk last night to remember they were together.

He throws another punch. This one catches my chin and has the room spinning more than it already was. Not good. My stomach turns, and when I shove him back, everything I drank last night comes back up.

On his feet.

Maybe it's time to stop drinking.

# JACE

*June—Four months later*

"Seriously?" I storm into the hotel room, tearing off the new Philadelphia Revolution hat that was placed on my head an hour ago, and throw it across the room.

My brother Max slams the door closed behind us.

We're both in Montreal, Canada, for the National Hockey League draft—something I've worked for my whole life. A fucking dream that came true today. Except my family took control like they always do and fucking ruined it.

Typical Kingstons.

"I asked you not to draft me. I begged you to let me go to another team. Any. Other. Team." I plant my hands flat against the window overlooking the city and try to get control of my anger, but I can't. "I did everything you asked me to do. I opted out of the draft last year, when you know I could have been drafted then. But no, you wanted me to get a degree, so I did. I graduated with fucking honors. Why the hell couldn't you just do this one thing for me?"

I watch his reflection through the window as Max calmly

11

folds his arms over his chest, careful not to wrinkle his custom Armani suit. He narrows his eyes, like he's looking at an ungrateful kid. "How about because it's our family's fucking team? How about because we wanted you close? Or maybe . . . just maybe . . . because you're the best center in the draft, and I paid a fuck-ton of money to get you on my team. *On our fucking team*. You ungrateful prick. The Revolution needed a center, and I wanted the best."

I tune out most of what he says and focus on one thing.

They wanted me close.

Of course, they did. I spent the first fifteen years of my life being the baby of the family. Then Dad died, and everyone thought they needed to take care of me, Max especially, since he became my legal guardian. When my little sister, Madeline, was born a few months later, I thought it would get better. But my brothers and sisters still think they need to parent me. They're never going to look at me like a grown man. Getting drafted to a different team was going to be my chance to get away.

"I'm the number one draft pick in the NHL, Max. My every move is going to be scrutinized. How much worse do you think it's going to be, now that I've been drafted by *my own family's team*?" My stomach churns, acid eating away at me, just thinking about what I'm up against. No one will ever take me seriously now. No matter what I do, I'm going to be a joke.

I haven't touched booze or drugs since that crazy night at the hockey house last February.

I've eaten clean.

I've stayed healthy.

I've stayed away from women. That one was harder than the others, but I fucking did it. And even with the seismic shift on our team, thanks to the strain between Sean and me, I still led the Kroydon University Knights to win the Frozen

Four championship, finishing the season as the Division One champs, and became the highest scoring player in the country. *The entire fucking country*. It was the best record Kroydon U ever had, and I was at the center of it.

Every professional coach wanted me.

*Everyone.*

I turn and face Max for the first time since he stood on stage after my name was called, holding a Revolution jersey, and I've never been so fucking angry. "I didn't want your help, *brother*."

"Well, you got it anyway. I just bought you for the next five years, Jace. And you're getting a big, fat signing bonus and a seven-figure-a-year salary. Suck it the fuck up, shithead." He pulls his phone from his pocket and stares at the screen.

"Gee . . . I'm sorry. Am I keeping you from something? Because you can feel free to get the hell out of my room, if I am."

Holy shit. I want to hit him. My fists clench at my sides.

Max looks from his phone to me, concern tugging at his eyes. "Sawyer needs you to call him. He says he's been texting you, but you're not answering."

"I guess I'm not. I was a little busy on stage being welcomed to the one team in the NHL that I don't want to play for." I leave off *asshole* at the end of my rant and flex my fists. *Again.* "What does he need?"

"Call him, Jace. Something's going on. He didn't say what."

And just like that, the tension in the room changes.

My brothers and sisters and I fight like cats and dogs, but when it matters, we've got each other's backs like no one else ever will. Even Max. Especially Max, when he's not being the arrogant asshole currently standing in front of me.

I pull out my phone and see seventy-two missed

messages. Most are congratulations on the draft. But it's the handful from my brother Sawyer and his wife, Wren, that have me concerned.

I've been staying with them since the fight at the hockey house. It made sense. I couldn't go back there... not after that shit show.

Why get my own place when I didn't think I'd be staying in Kroydon Hills after the draft?

I run my thumb across the screen and call Sawyer back.

"Hey, man. What's wrong?" I glance at Max, who's moved next to me.

"Jace . . . You've got to come home." There's static in the background as he turns down what I'm guessing is the music in his car.

"I have a flight back tomorrow. I'm supposed to do a few interviews tonight." Interviews I don't want to do, especially now. I can see how it'll go down.

*How does it feel to be drafted to your family's team?*

*Do you think you've been given special treatment because of your last name?*

*Do you think you earned the top spot?*

The call is breaking up, but I don't miss Sawyer's last sentence. "You need to take the jet back, Jace."

I look at Max, who flew in this morning on the King Corp. jet and put the phone on speaker. "You're on speaker now, Sawyer. Why do I need to take the jet back? What can't wait until tomorrow?"

"Just get home, little brother. We'll talk about it then."

Max clenches his jaw. "Spit it out, Sawyer. What's going on?"

"Wren delivered a baby yesterday . . ." Sawyer says quietly.

"Your wife's an ob-gyn. That's not exactly shocking," I tell him with a sinking feeling I've never felt before.

"Yeah well. Most moms don't leave the hospital the next day without taking their babies with them."

"Still not seeing why we need to take the jet home tonight, Sawyer." Max masks his concern with growing aggravation.

"Jace, come home. Now. The woman left the hospital. She left the baby. And she left a birth certificate naming you as the father."

My phone slips out of my hand and crashes to the floor.

$\sim$

*T*hree hours later, Max and I walk into Kroydon Hills Hospital, side by side. Everything that happened in the past twelve hours has been temporarily forgotten. Hell, everything that's happened in the past *twenty-two years* has been forgotten. Once we got on the jet, we called Sawyer back to get whatever details he had.

It turns out, the mom came in yesterday in labor. She didn't have insurance, and no one was with her. According to Wren, they think she gave a false ID. *If* the baby was full term, he was conceived in October.

*He.*

My son.

*Holy. Shit.*

My sister Scarlet meets us in the waiting room and wraps an arm around me. "Breathe, Jace. You look like you're about to pass out."

"Gee, Scar. I wonder why?" I shrug out of her hold and keep walking, right past the receptionist, who must know Scarlet because she doesn't stop me. I guess it helps that my family donates enough money to have their name on a wing of the hospital. "Where is he?"

Scarlet guides me to the maternity wing, then stops

outside a closed door. "He's inside with Wren." She meets my eyes, then runs a hand down my arm. "Don't forget to keep breathing."

I push through the door and grab the wall to stop my knees from buckling.

My sister-in-law sits in a rocker, holding a tiny baby boy wrapped in a pale-blue and white blanket. A matching beanie sits on top of a small head, and a little green pacifier that looks too big for his tiny mouth covers half his face.

Wren looks up as I step into the room. A delicate smile spreads across her face before tears well in her eyes. "Hey," she whispers.

I don't answer her.

I. Can't.

I move on instinct until I'm in front of Wren and the baby. *My baby.* That's when the quiet room starts closing in on me. The soft sucking of the pacifier grows louder as Wren stands and places the baby in my arms. *And holy shit.* I've held my nieces and nephews, some of them when they were only a few hours old.

But this.

Holding him . . . There are no words.

Scarlet moves behind me and tugs me down into the chair. "Sit, Jace. Wren needs to take some blood."

I run the tip of my index finger over the baby's beautiful little face and try to steady my racing heart. He looks so much like my sister Lenny's son did when he was born. I pull the soft beanie from his head and run my hand over the soft black hair sticking up.

"Jace . . ." Scarlet squeezes my bicep. "Let Wren draw blood, sweetie."

I look up at Scarlet, then over to Max, Sawyer, and Wren. "Does he have a name?"

"Cohen Kingston is what's on his birth certificate," Wren answers me.

"Jace," Scarlet cuts in harshly. "Don't fall in love yet. Let Wren draw blood. The lab will rush the results. Let's make sure this really is your baby, okay?"

"Do whatever you've got to do." Cohen opens his navy-blue eyes and looks up at me. "I don't need a test to tell me what I already know."

For the rest of my life, my world will revolve around my son.

# INDIA

*a*ugust – *One month later*

"She's knitting. That's never a good sign," Sophie stage-whispers to our friend Harper as they walk into the living room where I've been hibernating for two days.

"You better be careful. My Nana used to threaten to kill Big Daddy with her knittin' needles when he'd get fresh," Harper doesn't bother whispering before they drop down to the couch, sandwiching me between them.

I blow my hair out of my face, and try to remember the last time I washed it. "*She* can hear you."

Harper crosses her legs dramatically and leans back. "Could have fooled us. We knocked on the door and rang the bell. Care to tell us why you're ignoring us?"

"Not really," I mumble and keep counting my stitches.

Sophie places her hand on top of mine, stopping me. "What's going on, Indy? We know it's bad. Gramps called us in as reinforcements."

"Yup," Harper smugly agrees. "So spill."

*Knit one, pearl two . . .*

I continue to ignore them for another minute, but they both inch closer, waiting.

They know I'll cave to them. I always do.

Sophie and Harper were the first friends I made when I moved to town. The only friends, really. I met them the first time Gramps asked me to pick up desserts from Sweet Temptations, and they basically took pity on a heartbroken teenager and never let go.

"Fine." I put down my needles and yarn and close my eyes. "I didn't get the job. The one I interviewed for *three* times. They went with a teacher who had more experience." A bundle of frustration and fear clogs my throat. "It's almost the end of summer. Everyone has their staff in place. There're no more jobs to apply for within a fifty-mile radius. My loans have kicked in. My insurance just changed. And I'm broke."

"Indy . . ." Harper wraps an arm around my shoulders and squeezes. "You're amazing. You're going to find a job. Sometimes it just takes a while. I can't remember how many resumes I sent out after I graduated."

"And don't even look at me. I just keep racking up the student loans. One more year until I'm done. Then God only knows how long it'll take me to find a job. This is normal stuff, Indy. Can't Gramps help you with the loans?"

I bristle at her question. "I refuse to ask him. He's already done so much for me and Atlas. I'm not going to borrow money from him."

"You know . . ." Sophie says carefully, like she's walking through a mine field full of explosives, just waiting for one to detonate. "Amelia's brother is looking for a nanny."

Oh yeah. I'm going to explode. *A nanny?* Really?

"Doesn't your boss have seventeen brothers?" Harper teases.

I know it's not *that* many. I've gotten to know Amelia

Beneventi a little over the past few years, I've worked across the street from Sweet Temptations. She's got a ton of siblings. Maybe not seventeen, but more than the average person. None of that matters though. "I'm not a nanny, Soph. I've got dual degrees in early childhood education and childhood development. I'm supposed to be a teacher, not someone who changes diapers."

"I heard the pay is good," she challenges with a tilt of her head.

*Well.* That stops me in my tracks. "How good?"

"Let me get the number for you."

~

*I*'m sitting on my bed later that night, staring at the number I've typed into my cell phone and trying to force my finger to press the green call button, when Gramps knocks on my door. "Come in."

"Are you hungry? I just pulled chicken off the grill." With his arms crossed over his chest, he walks further into my room and tries to nonchalantly look at my phone. "How are you feeling?"

Atlas and I moved in with Gramps right after Mom died. It was my senior year of high school, and we were inconsolable. But he took us in, no questions asked, and did the best he could.

"A little better. Thanks for asking the girls to stop by. They helped." I look down at the phone and consider shutting it off.

"You'll find something soon, Indy. Don't give up." He leans down and kisses the top of my head. "Come on. Let's eat."

I look from him back to my phone and swallow my nerves. "I'll be down in a minute. I need to make a call."

He nods and walks out of the room as tears fill my eyes.

Am I really going to interview to be a nanny?

I mean, I love kids and babies. I spent summers working part-time at our local daycare, so I know I could do the job and do it well. The question is . . . do I want to?

I pull up the banking app on my phone and stare at the single-digit balance in my account.

Beggars can't be choosers, India.

With a press of my thumb to the screen, I dial the number and wait until a feminine voice answers.

"Hello?"

"Hi." I remind myself that my student loan payment is already past due this month. "I'm calling about the nanny position."

# JACE

"*J*ace, seriously. We've interviewed twenty-seven nanny candidates, and you've found something wrong with every single one." Sawyer bends down and tries to scoop a sleeping Cohen out of my arms, but I ignore him and close my eyes.

Cohen and I like to soak in the warm sun in the backyard. The sound of the waterfalls in the distance puts him right to sleep. Works like a charm every time. Which is a good thing because this little dude doesn't like to sleep. Probably because he doesn't like to be put down. *Ever.* "One of them hit on you in front of Wren, asshole. Am I supposed to leave my son with someone who only wants to nail a Kingston?"

"Okay, yes. *Some* of them seemed more interested in other things than Cohen but not all of them. It's time, Jace." He tries for the serious big brother tone, but fails.

Apparently, this is his attempt at a *Come to Jesus* meeting.

Ha. If he only knew.

"Your house is ready. Half the damn family lives on this street. If you need help, we're literally within walking distance. It's time, man."

"Great," I answer, sarcasm dripping thick like honey from my voice.

I've been crashing with Sawyer for a while now. He and our brother Hudson own half the houses in the lakefront neighborhood where both they, their wives, and our step-mother and little sister live.

When Cohen and I came home from the hospital last month, my siblings descended. All eight of them, along with my stepmother. By the end of the night, they decided I'd rent one of the properties down the street, and my sister Scarlet declared herself in charge.

I should have pushed back, but my fucking world had just imploded, and I was in shock.

Pretty sure I still am.

I didn't know the first thing about taking care of a baby, which is why we started looking for a nanny. Even though the idea of leaving a stranger with my kid makes me crazy.

My siblings have really stepped up and helped me with Cohen this summer. But we all have jobs and can't keep going the way we've been.

I need help.

The back door clicks shut, and my eyes pop open when Wren steps outside. She stops next to us and smacks the back of Sawyer's head. Then she opens her arms to me and waits as I carefully transfer Cohen to her and kiss the top of both their heads. "Favorite sister-in-law," I whisper.

"Hey," Sawyer whines. "You wouldn't let *me* hold him."

I shrug. "I like her better. She's not trying to kick me out."

"Nope. I'm not kicking you out, Jace. We love having Cohen and you here." She presses her lips to Cohen's fore-head. "But . . . I agree you need to hire someone. Whether you decide to move into your own house or not. We all need help."

"Not happening, Red. He's moving into his own house. I talked to Scarlet this morning. She said the house is finished and waiting for Cohen and you," Sawyer grumbles.

Nothing like knowing your family still thinks you're not capable of handling your own life. "I would have taken care of it myself."

Sawyer nods like he doesn't believe me. "I love you, jack-off. And I love my nephew even more. But I didn't plan on spending my first summer married to Wren while sharing a house with you. Time to man up."

I fucking hate that he's right.

They both are.

"Fine. When's the next interview?"

*~*

## India

"You're really going to interview for a babysitting job?" Atlas isn't *exactly* helping my nerves settle.

I turn down the tree-lined street with Kroydon Falls filling the horizon and take in the enormous lakefront houses. You could fit five of Gramps's tiny bungalows inside one of those monsters. "Listen to me . . . It's not my dream job. But not all of us have full rides to D1 schools. I have bills to pay. This job pays *well*. It's a live-in position with full health benefits. It's the perfect job to get me through until I can get the one I want."

"So you're gonna move in with some guy you don't know?" he throws back at me sharply.

I bite the inside of my cheek in an effort to stop myself from reaching through the phone and strangling my brother. "Jesus, Atlas. It's a job. *If* I get it, he won't be paying me to fuck him. He'll be paying me to take care of his son."

"Gross, Indy," he groans, and I smile triumphantly. "Just promise me you're not going to give up on what you want, and be careful," he lectures. "And call me later."

I love my brother and all his overprotective ways, but sometimes he's an asshole.

Instead of focusing on that, I try to center myself and visualize getting the job. I might not have imagined myself as a nanny, but it's got to be better than waiting tables at The Busy Bee for another year.

Carefully, I step out of the car and smooth my hands down my sleeveless sundress. I was going for professional but figured the lucky suit I've been wearing to every other interview might be a little too formal for this one. Besides, it's apparently not so lucky. Instead, I opted for a black sundress I got at the fancy secondhand shop that opened on Main Street a few months ago.

People in this town get rid of the nicest stuff.

It's a little less formal but still hopefully says *hire me*.

Please let it say hire me.

Please. *Please*. Please.

I try to appear calm as I walk along the stone path to the front door, just in case anyone is watching, then press the doorbell. A moment later, the door swings open and a beautiful redhead I immediately recognize greets me.

"Hi, I'm Wren. You must be Indy." She offers me her hand, then steps away and motions for me to come in. "Thanks for coming today. I'm helping Jace with the interview process."

"Thanks for having me?" It comes out more like a question than a statement.

But seriously, this woman was just in The Busy Bee a few days ago, talking with her friends about the multiple orgasms her husband had given her that morning. The group of them are regulars, and as much as I try not to pay attention to what customers talk about, sometimes it's hard to miss. My cheeks flame, just thinking about it.

She walks us into an oversized industrial kitchen and offers me a bottle of water before we both sit down.

"I'll grab Jace in a few minutes. But first, why don't you tell me a little about yourself, and then I'll fill you in on the job?"

Here goes nothing.

~

*B*efore I know it, I've given her the same speech I give in all my interviews, and I'm listening to what the job will entail.

Yes, the position is live-in.

Yes, the pay and benefits are incredible.

Pay off my student loans in a year *incredible*.

And have health insurance.

"When would the position start?"

Wren recaps her water bottle and smiles. "As soon as possible. Jace has been staying here since the baby was born. And I'm going to be sad to have them leave, but they need their own space. That's where you'd come in. He's a new dad and a little unsure of his instincts. He needs to get to work and needs more help than we can give him."

I nod. "I can understand that."

"So . . . are you ready to meet Jace and Cohen?" She stands, not waiting for my answer. "I'll just go grab the boys."

Ready as I'll ever be.

I sip my water and weigh the pros and cons of this job. It's not what I ultimately want to do, but it'll definitely more than work for now. I relax, knowing the decision has been made, then nearly choke when the *boys* in question walk into the room behind Wren.

These are not boys.

No.

These are men.

Two gorgeous men.

The one with messy brown hair throws a muscular tatted arm around Wren, then looks skeptically at me, while the man I assume is Jace Kingston stands by the door, swaying, with a tiny bundle wrapped in a gray and white muslin blanket on his shoulder.

Holy. Shit.

A man holding a baby has never done anything for me. But this man . . .

*This man, who's hopefully going to be my boss.*

Wait… this man that I'm pretty sure I recognize.

Where do I know him from?

"You," he says almost accusatorily. "I know you."

I tilt my head, studying him for a second as he takes a step forward, forcing me to look up. Oh. My. God. "You almost ran me over in front of Sweet Temptations last winter."

The baby in his arms whimpers, and he adjusts him, muscles flexing as he switches arms.

*Oh my.*

A sexy smile spreads across his face before he quickly masks it with indifference.

"Guys, this is India Monroe. Our *final* candidate for the nanny position." Wren arches a brow between both men. "She's also a waitress at The Busy Bee." A red flush works its way up her neck and face before she looks at me with a laugh. "I hope you'll try to forget some of the conversations I have no doubt you overheard between my friends and me."

I bite down on my bottom lip, trying to hide my smile, and nod. "Nice to officially meet you both."

"India . . . huh," Jace murmurs. "Sophie wouldn't give me your name that day."

I smother a laugh. "She's a good friend. She's actually the one who told me you were looking for a nanny."

"What are your qualifications?" His easygoing smile from a moment ago vanishes.

"Jace," Wren chides. "I told you. You should have just interviewed her yourself."

I push the folder holding my resume across the counter. "I have dual degrees in early childhood education and childhood development. I'm CPR certified, and I've got experience working at a day care."

"Why don't you introduce her to Cohen?" Wren nudges Jace, and he looks like he'd rather eat nails.

*Okay.* I think I'm getting this dynamic. She wants him to hire a nanny, but he doesn't want to give up control to a stranger. I can sympathize, but I want this job. Hell, I *need* this job. I take a tentative step closer and smile gently. "He's beautiful. How old is he?"

"A few days shy of two months old," he answers, still obviously trying to figure me out. "We'll need to do a background check."

"Scarlet already did one, Jace. I emailed it to you this morning," Wren taps her fingers on the folder I'm guessing holds a copy of my background check.

"Scarlet?" I question, not having heard anything about the baby's mom yet.

"Our sister," Sawyer supplies.

Okay then. I ignore the relief I feel, knowing she's not the baby's mom. But then, who is and why isn't she here? And why are his sister and sister-in-law dealing with all this instead of him?

Jace's eyes travel over me, and I'm not sure if he's shooting imaginary daggers my way or trying to picture me naked. "Tell me why you want to be a nanny with degrees like those."

"Honestly . . . I've been interviewing for kindergarten teaching positions. But there aren't a ton of them out there. I think this is something I'd be really good at. It's not exactly what I'd planned, but sometimes, you have to be willing to be open to what the universe puts in front of you." *Phew*. Please let me not have just fucked this up.

"I'd want a clause in your contract guaranteeing you'll stay for the entire season. I don't want to have to replace you halfway through if you find a teaching job. That's not fair to Cohen." His piercing blue eyes harden with the demand.

Can I guarantee him a year?

I think about the salary Wren and I discussed earlier and the health insurance that goes with it, and I know my answer.

"I can do that," I tell him, then drag my eyes over the tiny bundle tucked against his shoulder. One big hand spreads across the entire width of Cohen's back.

Jace looks from his brother to his sister-in-law, then drags his unconvinced eyes over me. "Can you sign contracts and move in this weekend?"

"Like tomorrow?" I squeak, knowing I'm going to say yes, and Gramps will kill me for bailing on my shift at the last minute.

"How about Sunday afternoon?" he offers, and I fight to contain my sigh of relief.

Holy shit. I got the job.

"Thank you. I appreciate this opportunity." If my smile grows any wider, I think my face would split wide-open.

Jace moves Cohen until he's holding him like a football, picks up the pen from the counter, jots his number and an address down on a note pad, then pushes it toward me.

Cohen picks that moment to spit his binky out of his mouth, and within seconds his eyes pop open. A few strands of dark hair stick out from under his hat near his temples, and tiny pink lips purse, probably holding back a scream that's about to break free but hasn't yet. But it's not until big blue eyes slowly blink and stare up at me, I feel my heart crack open for the second time in my life.

# JACE

*J*take a long look at the empty bedroom, making
sure I haven't left anything behind.

This house turned into a refuge for me after *that weekend*.

The one where I woke up so shitfaced I didn't know
where I was, who I was with, or what the fuck I was on.

My brother and his wife may not have officially offered
up the room, but after a few nights, Wren swapped out the
frilly pink sheets that were on the guest bed, and I came
home from hockey practice to blue flannel ones. She'd gotten
rid of the prissy white comforter too.

The message was received.

I was welcome to stay as long as I wanted, and I was more
fucking grateful for that silent statement than I'd ever been
for the nonstop talking of any of my siblings.

A knock on the door frame drags me from my thoughts
before Wren moves next to me, cradling a sleeping Cohen.
"I'm going to be sad when you're not here tonight, Jace." She
gently presses a kiss to Cohen's head, then hands him to me.
"Call, or hell . . . just come back if you need anything."

Her eyes well up with tears that threaten to spill over

when I pull her against me. "You saved my life, Wren. That night I found you on the side of the road after your car accident was one of the worst nights of my life. Then . . . seeing you hurt. If any one thing had been different, I could have easily been the cause of that accident. I could have killed somebody. I *could* have killed you. Finding you . . . *staying here.* I've never said it before, but you saved me from myself."

She shakes her head almost imperceptibly. "You saved yourself, Jace. Don't doubt your strength."

"You gave me a safe place to land when I didn't deserve one. My brother is a lucky man to have you. And if the fucker ever forgets it, you call me. I'll help you bury the body."

When the first tear falls, she laughs and tucks her face into my chest. "You're the little brother I never knew I wanted and now can't imagine my life without, Jace."

"Hands off my wife, jack-off." Sawyer pulls Wren away from me with a stupid grin until he sees her tear-stained cheeks. "What the hell did you do?"

Wren wipes her face and smiles. "Be nice. I'm going to miss them."

"They'll be three houses away, Red. Please don't cry." He looks between her and me, and I shrug as I leave the room.

"Hey, Jace," Sawyer calls out once I'm halfway down the hallway. "Fair warning. The whole family is coming over to the new house this afternoon."

Cohen picks that moment to wake up and cry.

Yeah, buddy. Pretty sure I want to cry now too.

~

My family is . . . I'm not sure exactly what we are. *We're something.*

Loud. Obnoxious. Fiercely loyal. And a complete shit

show most days. From the outside, we look like we've got it all together. From the inside . . . let's just say we've worked hard to be as well-adjusted as we are. And some days that's not really a term I'd use to describe us.

We've grown up in the public eye, and it's been a bitch. Everyone wants to nail a Kingston or use us for something. That's why we allow very few people into our inner circle. Most of us have enough trust issues to fill the football stadium that's made us famous.

I'm man enough to admit I do.

Nine siblings.

Six spouses.

One stepmother, who's only a few years older than me, and nine grandkids.

Ten now, counting Cohen. And they're all in my new house. Kids run in every direction. Glasses of wine and bottles of beer fill most of the hands that aren't holding babies.

My sisters are arguing over the way my kitchen should be set up. Like I give a shit where the utensils are in the triangle. When I told them I didn't see any triangles in the room, they all stared at me like some sort of hive mind, sharing one brain, and that brain thought I was an idiot, so I got the hell out of there.

My brothers are debating which room I should give to the hot nanny.

*Becket's words, not mine.*

Apparently, he heard it from Sawyer.

Not that they're wrong. Because she's a fucking smoke show. I knew it the first time I saw her in front of Sweet Temptations. Had things been different that weekend, I'd have probably searched her out after we won our game. But if there's anything I've learned over and over and fucking over again in my life, it's that you can't change the past.

That shit's set in stone. And that weekend changed everything.

"I think you should put her next to you, man." Becket smiles proudly like he just figured out the answer to world peace.

"Dude. Don't go there," I groan instead of telling them all to fuck off.

See? I've grown. The old me would tap a beer to his and bet on how long it would take me to get my hot new nanny into bed. The new, boring me has a bottle of water in my hand instead of a beer and is still trying really hard not to imagine what she looked like under her prim little sundress.

I can ignore the draw to her I felt yesterday . . . I don't have a choice.

Maybe if I tell myself that enough, I'll believe it.

"What are you guys talking about over here?" My sister Amelia joins my brothers and me, with Cohen sleeping soundly in her arms.

When this kid is held, he sleeps like a champ.

Put him down, and he revolts.

I'm so screwed tonight.

"Jace was just saying the new nanny isn't hot," Sawyer taunts as he eyes me over the top of his beer.

*Fucker.*

"I didn't say that." I glare.

"Because you're not blind," Amelia agrees, and we all stop and stare.

Her husband Sam's eyebrows shoot up as a predatory grin slides across his face. "Go on, Snow. Tell us how hot Jace's new nanny is," he pushes her. "Should I be jealous?"

"Listen." She rolls her eyes. "I happen to know Indy. She's worked at The Busy Bee for years and comes in to pick up the daily pastry order. She's a nice girl. Kind of quiet. She's been through a lot."

Becket folds his arms across his chest. "Being a nice girl doesn't make her hot, Amelia."

"No, Becks. But being five foot four with a tiny waist, tight ass, and big boobs does." We all stare at my sister with our mouths gaping. "Add in blonde hair and pretty, golden eyes, and she's hot, even if she tries to hide it." Amelia's eyes narrow. "And no, that doesn't mean you should be jealous, Sam. It means I can appreciate a beautiful woman. The fact that she's sweet and kind just makes her a good person." Amelia trains her eyes on me. "Which means she'll probably be great with Cohen. So don't mess it up by banging the nanny, Jace."

I raise my hands in protest. "Who said anything about banging the nanny?"

"Oh please. We all know you, kid," Becks taunts.

Max joins our growing group with a whiskey in hand. "What do we all know?"

"Pretty sure you know everything, don't you, Maximus?" I walk away and out the back door before he can answer.

I'm not sure when I'm going to get over him taking me in the draft, but it sure as shit hasn't happened yet.

After narrowly escaping the rest of the family, I control my urge to kick something, while at the same time resisting the craving to go back inside and grab a beer.

That one's a little harder.

Are all families as suffocating as mine?

~

*I*ndia

My phone rings again as I toss the last of my toiletries into my bag and zip it up. I don't even need to look at the phone to know it's Atlas. He's called all morning.

You'd think he'd get the hint, considering I haven't picked up once.

Not since I hung up on him yesterday.

"You gonna keep ignoring your brother?" Gramps asks as he moves into my room.

I add my bag to the suitcase lying open on my bed, then turn to stare down Gramps. "How do you know I'm ignoring him?"

The old man chuckles. "Because when you refused to answer his calls, he called me. *During the Sunday morning rush.* And he didn't just call me once, India. He called me nonstop until I answered. He said you're mad at him."

"Furious would be more like it." I try to close my suitcase, but apparently, it defies the laws of gravity or something because this sucker refuses to shut enough for me to zip it up.

*Hmm* . . . I climb on the bed and sit on it, then finally get the zipper to close and hop off, out of breath but proud of myself. "Atlas is a dumbass who doesn't get a say in my life, Gramps. I need a job, and I found one. There's nothing else to it."

"India . . ." He sighs. "Damnit." Gramps's voice softens as he steps in front of me and cups my cheek in his weathered hand. "You're more stubborn than your grandmother and mother combined. Remember, you'll always have a job at The Bee waiting for you. And if you need money, I can help you. You don't have to settle for this, if you don't want to."

"I know that." I try to reel in the sass that's on the tip of my tongue. He means well, which is more than I can say for my smart-ass brother. "I'm actually excited about this, Gramps. You and Atlas are just going to have to trust me. I know what I'm doing."

"I know you do." He pulls me against him. "You're broth-er . . . *ehh.* Some days, I think he's taken one too many hits to the head. But he's just being protective. I'd be disappointed in the man I raised if he wasn't."

I pull back and narrow my eyes. "Not fair. How am I supposed to be mad at him when you say something like that?"

Gramps picks up my suitcase and smiles. "I'm an old man, sweetheart. I know it's easier to catch a bee with honey than vinegar. Your brother will learn that one day."

"I love you, Gramps." I kiss his cheek and follow him to my car.

"Do you have your meds with you?" He places my suitcase in the trunk of my car and slams it closed with a little extra umph when I don't answer right away.

"Nope. I thought I'd live on the wild side, so I left them in the kitchen." I stare at him with a hand on my hip. "Of course I have them with me."

"Does he know?" Gramps asks pointedly.

"I'm not required to disclose my medical history to an employer." The warm and fuzzies I was feeling a minute ago evaporate. "And you know that."

Gramps is quiet for a moment, even if he's looking at me like there's something else he wants to say but knows better than to say it.

Good thing too.

He knows how I feel about this topic.

"Fine. Just don't forget, he might be a big, bad hockey player, but I served as a marine most of my life. I know plenty of ways to kill a man. Slowly. Quietly."

I hug him again, then get in the car. "I'll keep that in mind, if my new boss decides to wage a war."

Gramps shuts my car door and steps back.

"Just be careful."

I blow the old man a kiss and pull away, whispering, "I always am."

∼

*I*t was a lot easier to act confident in front of Gramps than it is now that I've pulled into Jace Kingston's driveway. I double-check the address he gave me, then look back up at the navy-blue shaker house that's only slightly smaller than the one I met him in for the interview. This one has a white, two-tiered wraparound porch with huge windows and pretty trim. It looks like it should be sitting on the banks of the Hamptons.

Definitely fit for a Kingston, even if it doesn't exactly scream bachelor pad.

But I guess Jace Kingston isn't your typical twenty-two-year-old bachelor.

Then again, what the heck do I know?

I debate on whether to bring my suitcase with me now or come back out for it later. I'm not sure either way will make this less awkward. So I wrench it out and drag it behind me, praying the wheels don't break before I make it to the front door, then relax slightly once I get there with no issues.

The door is yanked open before I'm able to knock, and a very shirtless, very frazzled-looking Jace stands on the other side, holding an equally frazzled Cohen. The poor baby is wailing.

"Help . . . *please*." Jace steps aside as I drag my suitcase through the door and shut it behind me. "He won't stop crying. I changed him. I've held him. I tried feeding him. Then he puked like he was two days into a three-day bender and needed to make room. I don't know what the fuck to do."

The pained expression on his face would almost be funny if it weren't for Cohen's pitiful cries. I follow Jace down the hall and into a huge open space. The walls are bare and white, with arching honey-wood beams framing the vaulted ceilings. He stops next to a beautiful pale-blue sofa and leans against the arm. "I swear to God, if I have to call my family on day one of being alone with my kid and tell them I don't know what I'm doing and I already screwed up, I'll never hear the end of it."

Dark circles I hadn't noticed during the interview line his exhausted eyes.

Eyes that are looking a little crazed at the moment.

"May I . . . ?" I reach my arms toward Cohen. "Why don't you let me take him from you?"

Jace's eyes flash with a hesitant, protective glare. "You've held a baby before, right?"

"You're kidding, *right?*" My nerves skyrocket. "Because I basically have my entire life packed in that suitcase, and I've taken all sorts of shit from my grandfather and brother about taking this job. If you're not sure you want me here, tell me now."

"Sorry," he mumbles, looking one step away from completely losing his shit. And when he clenches his jaw, I'm reminded this man is my boss, not my friend.

"Yeah. Me too. I just mean . . . you're going to have to let me hold Cohen sooner or later."

He very carefully places the screaming baby in my arms, then takes a step back.

"Hello, little man," I coo softly. His sweet face is scrunched up and bright red, ready to cry some more until I tug off the beanie covering his hair. Then I untuck the matching blanket that he's tightly wrapped in.

Cohen's wails begin to fade when he and I walk across the room to the wall of windows overlooking the lake. I drop the blanket and hat on the window seat, and prop him up on my shoulder, rubbing his back until the tears and hysterics stop and his now-stuttered breathing slows down.

"That's better," I say softly as we sway in the sun. "Were you too hot, little man?"

Jace's shadow falls over us. "How did you do that? He's been screaming all day."

Cohen's breathing evens out, and I look up at his daddy.

His extremely hot, extremely shirtless daddy.

The one whose broad chest and muscles look like they've been carved from stone.

*Oh my.*

"Umm. Well, babies can sense your energy. If you're stressed, they're stressed. And please don't fire me for saying this, but you seem . . ." I look him over again. Basketball shorts hang from lean hips. A dark spot drips from one leg, where I'm guessing some of the spit-up hit him. A sock covers one foot, while the other is bare. I'm pretty sure there's still vomit on those muscles I was admiring a moment ago. He's a mess. A hot mess, but a mess either way. "You seem stressed."

Jace groans, and the sound is deep and rumbly. "I *am* stressed. He hasn't slept through the night since we brought him home from the hospital. I'm exhausted. And *he's* probably exhausted. God, I have no fucking clue what I'm doing. How the fuck do people learn this shit? How did you know to do that?" He runs his fingers through his hair, then holds his hand up in front of his face.

It's wet.

Oh that's definitely more vomit.

This time, his groan sounds pained as he turns and walks away from us.

"Should we follow your daddy, or do you think he needs a minute alone?"

A slamming sound comes from the direction Jace just went, and I look at Cohen's heavy-lidded eyes. "Alone it is, little man. How about you and me get to know each other better?"

# JACE

*A*fter I wash my hands, I linger in the kitchen for a few minutes.

This wasn't how I expected today to go, but I'm not sure I've ever been more grateful for another human being in my life. I need a shower, a change of clothes, and about fifteen hours of sleep. Swear to God, I'd settle for thirty minutes of quiet.

But is it *too* quiet?

When I make my way back into the living room, my new nanny sits in front of the window with her eyes closed, basking in the late afternoon sun. She has her knees bent, leaving her flip-flop-covered feet planted on the bench with her bright pink toenails peeking out.

I've had a recurring dream about this girl for months. I'm not sure if it's because she's the one that got away or maybe if it's that she's the one I was supposed to find, but there was something about her that day back in February, and now she's sitting in my house, holding my baby.

Cohen leans against her bent thighs, his face turned

toward the warmth coming through the windows. Sound asleep. "How did you do that?" I ask, awestruck.

India's eyes pop open at the sound of my strangled voice. "I think he tuckered himself out before I got here." She stands up, and I get a good look at her for the first time since she walked in and I threw my kid at her in *Dad of the Fucking Year* style.

She's wearing a long-sleeved, white Penn State football tee with a fraying pair of cutoff jean shorts that make her toned legs look a mile long and cup one hell of an ass. Her bouncy blonde hair is pulled up in a ponytail with a blue ribbon tied in a bow around it. She's girl-next-door beautiful, and Amelia's warning about not banging the nanny rings in my ears, something about it souring in my stomach before I can push it aside.

"Do you want a tour of the house?" I offer, unsure of the protocol and not liking the uncomfortable vibe hanging in the air.

"How about we put Cohen down first? Then you can show me around and give me a feel for exactly what you're looking for, day-to-day." She smiles and her whole fucking face lights up. It's the kind of smile men go to war over, and it reminds me of the first day we met, before my life took a sharp turn toward the shit show I've fought hard to get through. Most days, I'm winning the fight, but days like today sure don't feel like it.

"The second you put Cohen down, he's going to wake up," I warn.

"Then where does he sleep?" she asks, confusion creasing her eyes.

"On me, mainly." I move into the foyer and pick up her suitcase. "Do you have anything else in your car you want me to grab for you?"

"Nope." She gives me another small smile, and I feel my

heart thawing. "That's it. My grandpa doesn't live far. I can always run home if I forgot anything." She takes a few steps, then stops. "He sleeps on you? You're not kidding?"

"*When* he sleeps," I add, then start up the steps. "Got any experience with that?" I step into the bedroom next to Cohen's and put her suitcase at the foot of the bed. It's not lost on me that it's covered in the white frilly comforter from my first few days at Wren's house. Such a little wise-ass. "This is your room. Cohen's is next to it."

She walks around the room, dragging the tips of her fingers over the whitewashed wooden dresser Scarlet ordered, then looks through the curtains. "The room is stunning. Thank you."

"Thank my sisters. They got everything ready. I just gave up my credit card." I step backward through the door and point to the next room. "This one's Cohen's."

She follows me into the room the same sisters made sure would be perfect for my son. They're pains in the ass, but damn, I love them.

India stands next to me, inspecting the room. "I see a crib. Any reason why you're not using it?"

"He won't sleep in it. We tried," I grumble.

"Okay. We can try a few different things." She spins around and stops in front of the window where the sun bathes her in a warm glow. "Do you have anything smaller than the crib? A bassinet or a Moses basket?"

"I'm pretty sure I've got one of those in my bedroom." We walk down the hall and into my room, then move next to the baskety thing on wheels I think Wren called a bassinet. "This thing?"

She pulls out the blanket draped over the edge of it and tosses it on my bed, then gently lays Cohen down in the basket and backs away slowly.

I blink once. Twice. A third time. Then I grab her wrist

and pull her out of the room, dragging her toward a big window at the top of the stairs. Another window seat mirrors the one in the family room below, and I sit us both down, completely shocked. "How did you do that?"

Her smile is back, bigger and prettier than before. "Some babies are picky. They like to feel like they're still in a small space, but don't always like being wrapped up like a burrito."

"Did you learn that in school?" I ask, desperate to know anything that will help my son.

Her silky-looking blonde hair falls around her shoulders as she shakes her head gently. "No. My mom was a temporary foster mom while we were growing up. She'd get the babies after their parents gave them up but before they could be placed with their forever families. Sometimes it was just for a night. Sometimes it was for a few weeks or months." She glances back to the open door of my room. "Do you plan on keeping that bassinet in your room? Or in Cohen's room? Or I guess, in *my* room?"

Shit. I hadn't thought about that. "We should probably put it in Cohen's room once he wakes up."

"Okay, great. There's already a monitor in there." She claps her hands together with a happy energy I'm too fucking tired to deal with. "So how do you want to use me?"

I smile slowly before I can catch myself.

I can think of so many answers to that question . . .

~

*I*ndia

As the words leave my mouth, I wish I could reach out and yank them back in.

*How do you want to use me?*

Oh. My. God.

I try to act like I didn't hear what I just said and run my

teeth over my bottom lip. "What I meant was you haven't told me what your schedule is and what you expect daily. Wren said I needed to be flexible once preseason practices start and more so once the season started. But she wasn't exactly sure what that would look like."

Stop talking Indy. *Stop.*

Would it be entirely inappropriate if I asked him to put on a shirt?

I probably wouldn't be the first person to find his chest distracting.

Tanned and toned and cut like stone.

Good grief. Is it hot in here?

"I think you and I are going to need to find our footing as a team over the next few days. Practice officially starts in two weeks, but I train in the off-season too. So I'm at the rink every day. Usually first thing in the mornings. I've got a few things I need to catch up on too." His stomach grumbles. "Like eating and sleeping and showering."

"Okay. I can handle that. How about I go unpack and listen for Cohen while I'm doing it. Once he's up, I'm going to move his bassinet into his bedroom, and we can go from there. Is there anything I need to know? Do you have him on any kind of a feeding schedule?" Judging by the look on Jace's face, I'm pretty sure the answer is no.

"Listen, India—"

"Indy," I interrupt. "The only time anyone calls me India is when I'm in trouble."

"Okay." One side of his mouth tips up in a sexy grin for just a quick second before it's gone. "Indy."

My name rolls off his tongue almost like he's tasting it, soft and smooth. Too smooth, damn it. I shouldn't like the way he says my name. This man is my boss.

*Yup.*

That's going to be my new mantra.

"The contracts are on the kitchen table. How about we go downstairs and sign them? Then we can get to the good stuff."

Well, that sure as hell wasn't what I was expecting. "Sure. Lead the way."

~

*T*he contracts are simple enough. It's everything Wren and I discussed during the interview, but with an ironclad NDA attached. I basically can't discuss anything I see, hear, or read about Jace, his family, or their businesses. I sign it and push it across the table to Jace, who adds his name, then closes the folder and leaves it on the counter.

"Listen," Jace grumbles. "I've been playing hockey all my life. I'm a team player. I'm used to working with people, but this whole setup is new to me. Hell, fatherhood is still new to me. Trusting someone with my kid doesn't feel right yet. I'm not even sure I trust myself with him most of the time. But I'm trying. I'm gonna need you to give us some time to figure it all out."

"I can handle that," I tell him. "I'm not much of a sports girl, but I work well with other people. Different kind of team, but I get where you're coming from."

He pulls a folded piece of paper from his pocket and pushes it my way. "This is a list of names and numbers. The pediatrician. My sister-in-law Wren—the one who inter-viewed you—is a doctor. If you're worried about something, call her. The rest of my siblings are listed here, but try not to call them for anything unless I die."

My eyes grow wide as my mouth hangs open. "Umm, okay?"

"Don't ask. They're a pain in my ass. They're probably all

going to stop by a lot over the next few weeks. Sorry about that, by the way. But if you're going to be here for the next year, you'll have to get used to them." He mutters something else I don't catch while my mind spins at the idea of having to deal with this many siblings. I flatten the paper and look it over. Wow. There's a ton of them.

"There's food in the fridge and the pantry. I've got a meal service coming twice a week. If there's anything you want, just let me know." He opens a cabinet and shows me Cohen's formula and bottles. "I'll get you a credit card to use if you need to get anything for Cohen. Or just tell me. We'll figure it out." He stops and looks toward the steps, then grabs a shirt from the back of a counter stool. "I'm going to take a shower while he's still sleeping. Feel free to show yourself around. I'm sure there's shit I'm forgetting, but try to bear with me while we figure it out, okay?"

I refold the yellow paper and slide it in my back pocket before he walks away. "I do have one question . . . Should I expect to see Cohen's mother?"

"Fuck if I know," he growls before stomping off.

Well, that answers nothing.

I wait a few minutes before following him upstairs, then stop in my new room. I stare at the bed and contemplate lying down for a hot minute before deciding I should unpack first. It's barely six o'clock, and I've been going since six this morning, when my shift started at The Bee. No sooner do I lay my suitcase on the bed and open it, than a tiny whimper floats down the hall.

When I get to Jace's bedroom, his door is shut. I knock hesitantly and wait for an answer as the whimpers grow louder.

I slowly push the door open. "Jace . . ."

With no answer, I tiptoe over to the baby and peek down at him. Big blue eyes stare back at me from an unhappy face.

"Hey, little man," I say softly, not wanting to scare him but hoping to avoid a full meltdown. "Did you have a nice nap?"

His little mouth opens wide, and there's a fifty-fifty chance he's going to wail or yawn.

I do an internal fist bump when it's a yawn and scoop him up. "See? That's not so hard. Now, let's change your diaper and see if it's time for a bottle." He rests against my shoulder as the bathroom door opens and steam billows into the bedroom.

Oh holy hell.

Shirtless Jace was something. But fresh-out-of-the-shower Jace—with a towel wrapped around lean hips and water droplets dripping down a solid eight-pack and trickling along those muscles on a man's hips meant to drive a woman wild . . . Well, this is a whole level of torture I've never experienced before.

I turn away quickly, mumbling an apology and hightail it to the door before stopping. "He was crying . . . We're just. I'm . . ." I turn my head and peek over my shoulder. "Sorry. I'm just going to change his diaper."

He lifts his eyebrows without saying anything, and I get the hell out of his room and hurry into Cohen's.

Maybe this is going to be harder than I thought.

# JACE

"*D*ude. It's weird as hell," I tell Becks the next day without taking my eyes away from the big window in the family room. *I can't.* They're glued to Indy dancing around my backyard with Cohen on her shoulder, her long blonde hair catching in the wind. "I don't know her, but I'm just supposed to trust her with Cohen." And the weirdest fucking thing is . . . I think I already do.

My instincts are warring with themselves. Part of me knows I hired her to take care of Cohen. The other part . . . Well, the other part needs to shut the hell up.

Becks leans against the back of the girly sofa Scarlet bought, holding the contract he came over to pick up. "Yup. Yet another reason I'm never having kids. Although, if the nanny looked like *that*, maybe I could be convinced."

The fucker is looking at Indy like she's the last piece of cake left on the table after a family dinner and he's ready to lick it so no one else can. That idea has no fucking business pissing me off the way it does. I shove his shoulder. "Stop looking at my fucking nanny like that, asshole."

"Hey." He shoves me back like we're kids again. "Amelia said *you* can't bang the nanny. She didn't say anything about *me*."

"What the fuck, Becket? Don't make me hit you." He might be the older brother, but his days of being able to beat me are long gone.

Becks's eyes narrow before he bites back a laugh and smacks me with the contract. "Whatever, jack-off. You've made it a whole twenty-four hours without fucking her. That's some kind of record for you, isn't it?"

I nod and keep watching the pretty girl holding my baby.

"Have you talked to Max yet?" When I don't answer, he groans. "You know you're going to have to get over this shit with him at some point."

"Get over the fact that I told him I don't want to play for *his* team and he drafted me anyway? I'm not a piece on a chess board for Max to manipulate." When I turn back to look outside, the sun is setting over my son, and I know I have to *be* better. Have to *do* better. I might be playing for the Revolution, but I'm the master of my own fate.

"I'll be the best on that ice. But I'm not doing it for Max. I'm doing it so no one can question my skill. I'm doing it so the story stays on my performance, not my personal life."

I'm doing it so Cohen can grow up here with his family.

Not because this is where I want to be.

This was my chance to get out from under the shadow of the Kingston name.

The door opens, and my pretty nanny walks in. A pink flush sits high on her cheeks as she presses her lips to Cohen's head before she sees Becks and me. "Oh, I'm sorry. I didn't realize you had company."

"This isn't company. It's my brother," I nod toward Becks as he steps forward and offers her his hand.

"Becket Kingston. At your service." *What a fucking tool.*

"Nice to meet you, Becket." An alarm goes off on Indy's watch, and she adjusts Cohen with ease, then silences it. "I'm going to give the little man a bath and a bottle and see if I can get him down for bed."

"You think it'll be easier tonight?" Sounds too good to be true, but maybe she's got some magic mojo I don't.

She runs the tip of her finger down the length of Cohen's nose until he scrunches his face and smiles. It's probably gas, according to my sisters, but I love when my kid smiles.

Indy looks back up at me with a beautiful smile on her face, brimming with enthusiasm. "That's the plan. Wish me luck."

I know I'm not supposed to notice that smile and wonder if that's what she would look like on her knees, but damn, it's hard.

Becks and I both watch as she walks out of the room and heads up the stairs. "Damn . . ." He whistles quietly. "I think I'm suddenly psychic."

"What the hell are you talking about?" My eyes trail Indy and Cohen until they're out of sight.

"Psychic. You know . . . like I can see the future. And I see a shit ton of cold showers and jerking off to that woman in your future, little brother." He claps my back. "Have fun with that."

I don't bother correcting him.

He's not wrong.

I should have thought about that before I hired her.

~

*I*ndia

After a bath and a bottle, Cohen went to sleep in his room a tiny bit easier than yesterday. He slept like a champ for a few solid hours.

At least until he woke up, thinking it was playtime.

Well, game on, little man . . .

I've just gotten him back down for hopefully a longer stretch of time when I step into the hall and walk directly into a brick wall. Jace's hands brace me, giving me a sense of déjà vu, while a swarm of butterflies take flight in my stomach. "Sorry."

When he drops them to his side, I swallow back my surprising disappointment at the loss of contact.

*What the hell?*

He's changed into sweats and an old t-shirt. There shouldn't be anything special about the way he looks, but oh my, he wears it well.

His eyes move to Cohen's closed door. "Did he go back to sleep?"

"Yeah. I changed him and got him back down faster than I was expecting. He wanted to party but couldn't hang," I tease.

Jace's eyes singe my skin as he looks at me, not bothering to hide his stare.

My best guess is he hasn't decided whether he likes me yet. "I'm heading to the basement to work out for a while."

"Okay. I'm going to bed. But I've got the monitor." I hold it up in my hand awkwardly, then internally cringe. I'm not a self-conscious person by nature. But I swear, something about my new boss brings it out in me. "Good night."

I hurry into my room and shut the door, then lean back against it.

I can handle the baby.

His daddy, on the other hand, has me tripping over myself *already*.

My phone rings, and I dive for it on the nightstand, not wanting the noise to wake Cohen, then sigh when my brother's face flashes across the screen. "Hey," I answer and climb into bed.

Atlas's dark pissed-off eyes stare back at me. "You *are* alive," he mocks. "You see, I wasn't sure since I've been calling *for two days*, India. And you haven't answered once."

"Maybe if you didn't call ninety-two times like some kind of crazy stalker, I'd have answered." Okay, so maybe it wasn't quite ninety-two times, but it was enough. "And since when do you call Gramps if I don't answer the phone?"

"Since when do you not answer the damn phone?" He clenches his jaw, and I remind myself I love my brother even when he's an asshole and choose to keep my mouth shut. "How was I supposed to know you were all right? Something could have happened to you."

"Listen, little brother. You knew I had a shift yesterday. You know what The Bee is like on Sundays. You also knew what the rest of my day was going to look like, just like I knew you had classes and practice today, so I didn't bother calling you back when I knew you were busy."

"Whatever. I guess that means you moved in?" Atlas adjusts the screen before his roommate, Nate, pops into view.

"Hey, Indy. When are you gonna let me take you out to dinner?" he asks before Atlas elbows him away.

"She'll go on a date with you when hell freezes over, shithead."

"Atlas . . . Be nice," I scold.

Nate is like an excited puppy who still needs to be house-trained.

Totally harmless, but he's never taking me on a date, whether Atlas approves or not.

"Yes. I'm all moved in. So far, so good." I lay my head back on my pillow and mentally prepare myself for the fight I know I'm about to have with my brother.

"I still don't like this, Indy." He grabs a beer from the

fridge and pops the cap. "Make sure your boss knows you've got a brother who'll fuck up his world if he messes with you."

"I'm his nanny, Atlas. I'm here to take care of his son. That's it." I shake my head and try to ignore my brother's overprotective ways. He's always been like this. More so since Mom . . .

"Yeah well, you and Gramps are my world, Indy. If he fucks with mine, I'll fuck with his."

"Don't you have a game to worry about?" I try to change the subject. Atlas is usually pretty happy to talk football.

"Season starts next Saturday. We have a bye-week after that, and I'm thinking I need to come home. See my sister. Maybe intimidate her boss."

"I don't know what my weekends look like yet, but I'll check with Jace."

Atlas's jaw tightens. "I still don't like this, Indy."

"Well, I do, and I signed a one-year contract. Time to get over it. I love you, little brother. Now let me get some sleep before Cohen wakes up again, and I'm dealing with two babies."

"Are you calling me a baby?"

"If the diaper fits. Love you." I end the call, plug the phone into my charger, then check to make sure the monitor is on.

Fingers crossed I can catch a few hours of sleep before the little guy wakes up or Atlas calls back.

~

*T*he soft early morning light filters through the curtains the next morning when I walk into Cohen's room to calm the crying baby. "Shh . . . It's okay," I hum as he works himself up into a fit. "You did such a good job staying in your bed last night, handsome man. Let's change your diaper, then get some breakfast, okay?"

"You expecting an answer?" Jace asks as he steps up behind me, and a shiver runs down my spine.

"My God, you scared me." I spin around to face him and try to calm my shaky nerves, but oh my . . . he sure does make it hard. Dressed in another pair of basketball shorts and a t-shirt with the sleeves cut off, my new boss is panty-meltingly hot. I've never been much of an arm girl before, but Jace's arms could have Pinterest boards dedicated to just them. Talk about arm porn.

"Sorry," he chuckles, then takes Cohen from me and presses his lips against his head before lying him down on the changing table.

I grab new clothes from the drawer and lay them next to him, then cross my arms, trying to act cool instead of awkward . . . And maybe trying to hide the fact that my nipples hardened as soon as his breath hit my neck. "I wasn't expecting an answer, by the way. I just like to talk to him. I want to get him comfortable with my voice."

Jace laughs, and the sound is deep and rough and sexy as hell. It's the kind of sound that vibrates through you, warming you from the inside out. This man should definitely laugh more often. "Whatever you say." His fingers brush against mine when he hands Cohen back to me, and I suck in a quick breath as a frisson of electricity dances across my skin.

Jace must notice it or at least my reaction to him because he steps back with a glare. "I've got to go for a run, then head to the rink today. Will you be okay?"

I look down at Cohen. "Yup. The little man and I are going to have a great day."

Jace nods slowly, like he's not sure he believes me. "Call if you need anything."

Once he's gone, I lift Cohen up in front of my face and

smile. "Listen, buddy. Could you please not make a liar out of me?"

My new favorite little man's face pinches tight before he opens that cute little mouth and cries.

Okay. I've clearly got my work cut out for me.

# JACE

"*C*ome on, Kingston. You're moving slow as shit today."

I stop on the line, sweat dripping down my face and muscles already burning.

Connor Callahan, my new team captain, is standing on the side of the ice, leaning on his stick, and watching me.

"You like watching, Cap?" I push off and skate over to him, snowing him as I stop. "I'm sure I could find you something better to watch," I taunt.

"Fuck off, Kingston. Coach O'Doul asked me to stop by and check on you. Said you've been in here early every day for the last two weeks. You too good to wait around and skate with the rest of us?"

"Nah, man. I've just got stuff going on at home. Earlier works better for me. Gotta get it in when we can, right?" I remember being so fucking excited when Max got Connor on this team two years ago.

I might be pissed I'm playing for Max, but the Revolution will always be *my* team. You know the one. You watch them

59

as a kid and imagine yourself playing with the giants of the sport. It's still fucking surreal.

Connor looks at the snow on his legs, then back to me. "You gonna have your *stuff* taken care of when preseason starts next week?"

"This you asking? Or Coach?"

He drops a puck on the ice. "It's your captain asking, rookie." He shoots it to the corner of the rink. "Best two out of three. Loser buys lunch. Winner's choice." And he takes off before I realize what's happening.

I fly across the ice and battle it out with him in the corner, reminded why Connor Callahan is one of the best in the league.

~

*A*n hour later, I follow Connor into the place across the street from Sweet Temptations. He takes a seat at the booth in the back and shoves a menu across the table at me. "You ever eat here? They've got the best sandwiches around. It's the rolls."

A picture hanging above him catches my attention. Two kids stand on either side of an older couple. There's something familiar about them, especially the young girl. "Little early for lunch, isn't it?"

"Never too early." He closes his menu and taps his knuckles against the table. "So what's your deal, rookie?"

"What do you mean?"

"You just went number one in the draft. You've been practicing all summer but never with the team. I've seen you. You're lightning fast, not scared to fight it out, and your brother owns the team. So how come every time I've seen you, you look like someone pissed in your Cheerios?"

A blue-haired server stops next to us with an order pad in her hand. "Hey, Connor. You want your regular?"

"Yes please, Gladys." He winks at the older woman, then the fucker kicks me under the table. "What are you getting, rookie?"

I look from him to her, then back at the menu. "Ahh . . . I'll have what he's having."

She jots something down and smiles at Connor. "All right, boys. Be back in a minute."

"So . . ." he pushes.

"So what?" I ask just to piss him off.

"Cheerios. Piss. Explain." Gladys comes back with two chocolate shakes and places them on the table before leaving again.

"Seriously?" My mouth waters as I look at the shake. "Doesn't scream healthy."

"Watch and learn, rookie. You thought college hockey was tough. But it's got nothing on the pros. O'Doul is gonna work you so hard, you'll drop five pounds before our first game. You're gonna struggle all season to keep weight on. I spend my off-season trying to bulk back up before the next season starts. Now, answer the fucking question." He pushes a shake my way, then throws the straw at me.

"Nobody pissed in my Cheerios. I've just got some family shit going on." I take a drink and try not to chug the whole thing, it's so fucking good. "It's personal."

"Well, whatever it is, you need to get over it." Connor's glare darkens. "O'Doul brought you in for a reason. We won the cup last season, then had our goalie and top scorer retire. You're here to fill a damn spot, so we can win it again. Leave the personal shit at the door. We don't care whose kid you are."

"Max is my brother, not my dad." My fists flex under the

table. "How is it possible you don't know this? It's been everywhere for two months."

"Of course I know, rookie. We all fucking know." He looks less than impressed. "I was testing you. And you failed."

"Failed what?"

"Controlling your anger. You gotta mask that shit before you fuck up. Reporters are gonna come at you, and you need to be ready to deal with them better than you just dealt with me." He leans back as Gladys returns again, two big plates of burgers and fries in hand.

"Try being in my shoes, then tell me not to be angry. You were drafted at eighteen and called up the next damn year. Nobody was controlling you. You sure you wanna give me advice?"

"Listen, you spoiled little rich shit. You were drafted into the best damn team in the league. We won the fucking cup when no one thought we would. And we did it after your brother and O'Doul rebuilt a team that had spent a decade losing." He takes a bite of his burger and takes his time before he leans across the table and lowers his voice. "Get the fuck over yourself and get on board. Most of us had to fight our whole lives for the opportunity to play for O'Doul. We'd do anything for Coach. You gotta get the solid-gold chip off your fucking shoulder and get on board before the rest of the team decides you're not worth it and ices you out. It's really hard to score when no one passes you the puck."

I shove my burger in my mouth before I can say something I shouldn't to my captain.

That's how they're all gonna see me.

A spoiled rich kid whose brother bought his spot.

*Fuck.*

"I don't care how good you were in college. You're playing in the pros now, and we fix our shit in-house." He leans back like he didn't just put me on my ass and finishes his burger. "Take a few days off and get your shit together. I want to see you on Monday. Be at the rink at ten. *With the rest of us.* Meet your new brothers before the preseason starts."

Message received.

"And rookie . . . Try to remember something, will ya?"

"Yeah?" I wait, not sure what other fucking nugget of wisdom he's going to try to shove down my throat.

"I'm not sure about you, but for most of us, we're living our dream. We're getting paid to play the greatest game that ever existed. When someone shoves a camera in your face, remember that. Only give them what you want to give them. You control what they see." He pops a fry in his mouth and chews slowly. "And when fans are waiting outside the rink after practice next week—because they *will* be—you sign whatever they put in front of you with your name and number. Make sure they can read it, and make sure you thank them. They're why we get to be here, living that dream."

"I'm not an asshole," I shoot back, pissed as hell.

Calmly, Connor runs another fry through his ketchup. "Good. Prove it next week."

~

*W*hen I walk back into my house that afternoon, it's quiet.

Too quiet.

My kid is never this quiet.

Not unless he's sleeping, which I'm still shocked he did in his own bed last night. Maybe Indy can sprinkle some of that fairy dust she must have hiding somewhere my way because I slept like shit. I guess I've gotten used to Cohen sleeping on me. Or maybe I've gotten used to sleeping in a chair holding him instead of in a bed. Hell, maybe I've just gotten used to not sleeping at all.

I'm not sure which it is, but all of the above, combined with the fact I've been fantasizing about my nanny since the day I met her, equal me sleeping like absolute shit.

I find the two of them when I step out into the backyard. Indy has a white blanket lying on the grass, and Cohen is on a colorful activity mat on top of it. Brightly colored zoo animals hang over his hand, and his feet kick in the air. And he's laughing as she squeezes his chubby thigh.

His first laugh. And she got it.

I'm not sure how long I stand there watching them before Indy notices me. That gorgeous smile crosses her face without hesitation as she waves me over. "Do you wanna show Daddy your new trick, little man?"

Cohen laughs again when Indie blows a raspberry on his foot, and my heart soars, then sinks.

I thought this was what I'd have one day.

A beautiful wife and family to come home to.

I just thought it would be years from now.

When I was set in my career.

When I had a fucking clue what I was doing.

Not when I was twenty-two.

Instead, I've got a baby who likes his nanny more than me. A nanny I can't stop thinking about in all sorts of ways I shouldn't. And I'm playing for my all-time favorite hockey team. The one team I didn't want to play for. A team who thinks I'm an asshole before they've even met me.

Time to fix this shit.

I've got to do better for him.

I kick off my sneakers and drop down next to Indy, then palm Cohen's belly and push words out of my suddenly dry mouth. "He's laughing."

She absolutely beams up at me. "He sure is. He's early.

Most babies don't laugh until they're closer to four months old."

I pick Cohen up and enjoy the way he burrows into my chest. It really is the greatest feeling in the world. Even if it's not how I envisioned it, this is my life. *Cohen's* life. And it's a good life.

I take in a deep breath, inhaling his clean baby scent, and my entire body relaxes.

I've been running on empty since the day he was born. Stressed and frustrated. Not knowing what the fuck I was doing. Spiraling again after months of feeling good about my life and my choices.

Fuck this shit.

I'm the master of my fate . . .

I stand and offer Indy my hand. "Want to get out of here?"

~

*I*ndia

Jace Kingston gives off hot and cold vibes like it's his mission in life. It's barely been forty-eight hours since I've walked through his door, and this man can't decide if I'm on his team or I'm his enemy. He might think he's hiding it, but he's doing a lousy job.

I don't think it's me though. I think he's struggling with something. I just don't know what. I'm a big believer in things happening for a reason. I've clung to that for years. Thinking there was a reason for the hell I've gone through has made accepting my life easier. I have to believe there's a reason and that I'll understand it and maybe even appreciate it . . . *eventually*.

Maybe I'm not just here to help Cohen.

Maybe I'm here to help his daddy too.

With that thought in mind, I let Jace pull me to my feet.

"Sure. Just let me grab a bag for Cohen. Where are we going?"

His steely-blue eyes hold my gaze, seeing too much, like he's looking directly into my soul. It's unnerving. "Have you ever felt like you were suffocating, Indy?"

An unequivocal *"yes"* falls from my lips quietly.

I want to tell him *if he only knew*. But this isn't about me.

"I need to get the hell out of this town for a few days. My family has a beach house about an hour from here. It's private and quiet. No family. No hockey." The exhaustion he was wearing yesterday is back. But today, it's different. The cracks are deeper. "We can bring whatever we need for Cohen. We all use the place, so there's tons of baby stuff down there already. Two nights. Three max. I've got to be back Monday for practice. But I could use the distance from this place."

He needs this, and I need this job, so I guess I need this too.

"Okay," I answer, a little more enthusiastically than I actually feel. "Give me half an hour, and I'll pack bags for Cohen and me. Could you grab his bed please?" I start creating a mental checklist of everything we'll need.

Nothing like being thrown into the deep end my first week.

"Yeah. I'll get the bed, bottles, and formula. Basically, I'll get whatever we need from the rest of the house. You focus on his room. Sound good?" Jace smiles, and it's hesitant and shy and so fucking sweet, I want to swoon right where I stand.

Damn him.

Falling in love with Cohen was unavoidable.

Falling for his daddy is out of the question.

*I*t's closer to an hour later when we load up in an SUV.

"What happened to the fancy sports car?" I tease after Jace buckles Cohen's car seat into the back of a mammoth black Maybach.

He takes the bags from my hands and places them in the trunk next to Cohen's bassinet and a clear, square, ten-gallon tote full of just about every other possible baby item this man could possibly own.

And they say women overpack.

"I got an eight-pound, two-ounce surprise. One that was safer in this one than that one." Then he winks, and good lord, he's unfortunately sexy. At least for me. *Employee*, I remind myself. *I'm his employee.*

"I didn't get rid of it though. It's in the garage. I fucking love that car." Jace catches me off guard when he places his hand on the small of my back. Goosebumps cover my skin as he guides me to the passenger-side door, opens it, waits for me to sit, and buckles my seatbelt before he closes the door behind me.

*Was that normal?*

Because I've had dates who haven't done that.

Of course, Gramps was usually watching when I left, and I got an earful when I got home about how those boys weren't worthy of my time. But still . . . Those were dates who I'm sure were hoping to at least cop a feel at some point.

Not the man I work for.

Not the one whose son has already stolen my heart.

Once Jace gets in and starts the car, he points at the digital sound system screen. "Shotgun controls the radio on road trips. You up for it, Indy?"

"Oh, I'm up for it," I laugh.

"No Taylor Swift though." We pull away from the house while he lays down the law.

"What do you have against T. Swift?" I ask as I scroll through my options.

"Wren secretly loves her. I've heard enough of her to last a lifetime," he grumbles and lowers his mirrored aviators, hiding his gray eyes from me.

But when I find "Wildest Dreams" and turn it up, I feel the death stare coming from him. "Sorry," I squeak with a smile, but I don't change the song.

"Sure you are." He tosses me his phone. "Want to place the grocery delivery order for us?"

I pull up the app on his phone and start adding to the cart. "What do you feel like eating?"

By the time we're crossing the bridge into the tiny shore town an hour later, I've learned Jace loves meat and potatoes. He's not into sushi. Hates carrots. Loves apples and peanut butter. And his face should be on one of those "Got Milk?" billboards. We're going to be here for three or four days, and we ordered a gallon each of skim and chocolate milk.

I crack my window and breathe in the thick, salty marsh air along the back bay and enjoy the happy memories that come with it. When we were young, Mom would bring Atlas and I down to visit Grams and Gramps each summer, and we'd all go to the beach for a few days. This smell . . . This smell brings it all back.

Before she got sick.

Before life got complicated.

I close my eyes and lay my head back against the seat.

My mind clears, and my muscles relax.

Maybe Jace isn't the only one who needed to get away.

~

*J* hadn't realized I'd fallen asleep until Jace's voice interrupts my dream, effectively tossing a bucket of ice-cold water over my body.

I look around quickly, seeing I'm still in the car, not in a bed. And my boss is sitting next to me, not crawling his way up my naked body. Holy hell. That dream was . . .

"We're here."

I look out through the windshield at the mansion in front of me. "That's not a beach house, Jace. That's an Italian villa."

"Yeah. Max, Sawyer, and Scarlet's mom designed this house a long time ago. Adeline has never been understated."

Judging her solely by the house in front of me, I completely agree.

I unbuckle and turn in my seat to check on Cohen, and my new buddy is still sound asleep. "I think he might have a hard time sleeping tonight after that nap." I get out and open the back to unbuckle Cohen's car seat while Jace grabs our bags from the trunk.

When we step inside, I'm slightly overwhelmed by the vast size of this place. "This is beautiful." Soaring ceilings and whitewashed wood flooring give an open feel to the inside of this beautiful house. Pale linen curtains cover floor-to-ceiling windows overlooking the beach and ocean. An over-sized, overstuffed white sectional sofa—big enough to seat a football team or maybe just big enough to fit the entire Kingston family—anchors a stunning living room.

It's much homier inside than the outside looks.

"Thanks. My mom redecorated when we were little, and no one has really changed much since." His voice changes when he mentions his mom, and I make a mental note to ask him about her one day. "How about I put our bags in the rooms upstairs and show you around? Then I'll grab Cohen's bed and the bin with all his stuff."

"Sure. Second new house this week. No big deal. Just don't be mad later when I have no clue where the heck I am, okay?"

He laughs like I'm kidding, but I've already forgotten what I've said as I put Cohen down and walk over to the French doors opening to a gorgeous infinity pool before the world falls away, and the sand and ocean come into view in the distance. "Wow, Jace. That view is magic."

"Yeah." He moves next to me. "It's beautiful."

When I turn, he's not looking outside.

He's looking at me.

Like he wants to kiss me.

And in this moment, I don't know if I have the strength to stop him.

Jace leans in as my watch beeps and breaks the spell.

*Oh my.*

That was . . . something. Close? Disappointing?

Almost the hottest moment of my life?

God, that's just sad.

As all these thoughts assault me at once, Jace tucks a stray lock of hair behind my ear and my knees threaten to buckle. *Because. Of. My. Boss.* "Do you need to get that?"

"Yeah. I do." Saved by the beep. "Could you show me to my room, please?"

I just got the reminder I needed that this isn't my life.

This isn't my man or my family.

I'm not sure if that's even in the cards for me.

# JACE

$\mathcal{O}$nce I show Indy her room, I grab Cohen and head into my parents' old bedroom. I should probably wake him, but he's still snoozing in his car seat, so I sit him down and walk out onto the balcony. The ocean waves crash against the rocks below, and the seagulls hover over something in the distance. I wrap my hands around the black wrought-iron scrolled railing and close my eyes.

What the fuck was I thinking?

I was going to kiss her.

I haven't kissed anyone in six fucking months, and I was going to kiss my son's nanny.

My phone vibrates in my pocket, and I think about just shutting it off.

Ignoring the world and unplugging.

When I pull it from my pocket I see twenty-one missed messages, and regret not doing it.

Two are from Connor and one from my agent.

The rest is my family.

No surprise. Our family group chat is enough to drive a saint to drink.

Thank fuck, I'm stronger than a saint.

SCARLET

Jace Joseph Kingston. What the hell are you doing at the beach house?

SAWYER

He's where?

SCARLET

At the beach house.

SAWYER

Like New Jersey?

HUDSON

I'm almost scared to ask.

LENNY

I'm not. Scarlet, how the hell do you know he's at the beach house?

MAX

Do you guys seriously not know she's got an app on her phone and we're all connected to it?

AMELIA

I knew.

SCARLET

That's because your husband is the only person scarier than me.

SAWYER

What the hell kind of app is it?

MAX

It's an app that tracks where you are and how fast you're driving.

HUDSON

Scarlet . . . What the actual fuck?

LENNY

More like HOW the actual fuck?

SCARLET

All your phones are on the King Corp. account, people. It wasn't that hard.

AMELIA

Mine isn't.

SCARLET

And that's why you know it's on there, little sister.

LENNY

OK. Not sure how I feel about this. But let's put a pin in that for a minute.

SCARLET

Consider it pinned. We're all looking at you, Jace. What the hell are you doing?

JACE

You know this isn't how normal families act, right?

HUDSON

Who wants to be normal when you can be awesome?

SAWYER

Keep telling yourself that, Huddy.

HUDSON

Fuck off, Huck Finn.

SCARLET

Focus, children.

JACE

I'm taking a few days off the grid. Cohen and Indy are with me. I've got everything we need and can Instacart whatever I don't have. I'll be home this weekend.

MAX

Practice starts next week.

BECKS

I don't know if I'd call the beach house off the grid.

LENNY

Sounds like a romantic getaway to me. But what do I know? It's football season, and I have a toddler. A quickie in the laundry room is a romantic getaway these days.

SCARLET

And that's how you ended up pregnant again.

LENNY

What can I say? The spin cycle makes it extra fun. You should try it.

HUDSON

Stop. Please. Dear God, Stop.

BECKS

Are you planning on trying out the spin cycle with Indy, Jace?

AMELIA

No nailing the nanny.

JACE

You guys are insane.

I wanted a few days of peace before training camp starts. That's it. I'll see you all next week.

And before anyone else gets a chance to answer, I shut off my phone.

Off the grid sounds really good right now.

"*S*o . . ." I take the potatoes and corn off the grill, then look over my shoulder at Indy, who's sitting at the long teak table behind me. The orange sun setting in the distance bathes both Cohen and her in a golden light that makes me itch to grab my camera, but I don't want to move. Instead, I pull out my phone and snap a pic of them, then shove it back into my pocket before she looks up. "The strangest thing happened earlier today."

"Oh yeah? Stranger than your new boss kidnapping you?" She chews on her bottom lip, and I fight the urge to press my thumb right where her teeth are pressing down.

Damn. I don't think this woman has the first clue how sexy this whole girl-next-door thing she's got going on really is. But fuck me . . . it is. Her hair is tucked in a messy knot on top of her head. A pale-blue t-shirt does nothing to show off her figure but somehow still looks fucking hot. And another pair of cotton booty shorts barely cover her toned thighs.

I turn back around and try to discreetly adjust my hard dick before I plate the stakes and set them on the table. "Yeah. I had lunch at The Busy Bee." Her eyes grow wide for a second before she chews on that damn bottom lip again. "Funny thing. It's been across the street from my sister's bakery for years, but I never ate there before. And then I sit down, and there's this picture on the wall."

Indy's face flushes a pretty pink as she adjusts Cohen in her arms. "Stop," she pleads.

"Come on. You were a cute kid. Who was the big guy?" I suddenly want to know everything there is to know about this woman in front of me. And not from the dossier Scarlet had put together either.

"That's my brother, Atlas. Eleven months younger, but he's always been twice my size. He's also ridiculously opinionated and overprotective. Actually . . . He's going to be home in a week. Would it be okay if I invited him to the house?" She cleans Cohen up and buckles him into the swing next to her.

"Sure. It's your house for the next year too. I want you to feel comfortable there."

"Thank you." Her eyes narrow, but her smile grows. "My turn to ask a question."

"Okay, shoot."

"You've lived in Kroydon Hills your whole life, right?" When I nod, she purses her lips. "How was today the first time you've ever been inside The Bee?"

It's my turn to be embarrassed. "I was never big on eating out. I'm still not. No matter how I answer this, I'm going to sound like a pompous douche."

She points her knife at me before she cuts her steak. "Come on. Now you *have* to tell me."

"I don't like to eat out. I hate feeling like I'm on display, and growing up a Kingston meant we were *always* on display. People felt entitled to us. They were always watching, and we always had to be on our best behavior. Which we never were, so we always got in trouble. Eventually, it was just easier not to go. I want to make sure Cohen never feels like that." I look over at Cohen, whose big blue eyes are getting heavy as he sways in the swing with his favorite plush hockey stick tucked under his arm and a matching cotton Revolution onesie and beanie. Completely innocent.

"That little boy is lucky to have you."

I make a sound in my throat, and Indy looks up at me through long lashes. "Do you want to know what drew me to this job?" When I look at her skeptically, she shrugs and presses her lips together, holding back a laugh. "Besides the solid paycheck, obviously. It was how protective you were of him during our interview."

"Was your dad protective of you and your brother?"

"Not at all. He left right after Atlas was born, and we never saw him again. My mom raised us with some help from my grandparents. They're the ones who own The Busy Bee. Well, Gramps does. Grams died a few years ago." She pushes the potatoes around on her plate, refusing to give me her eyes.

Okay, so she doesn't want to talk about her grandparents. Well . . . probably just her grandmother. Got it. "Does your mom live in Kroydon Hills?"

"No. She died a little over five years ago. That's when Atlas and I moved in with Gramps." She tries to put on a strong front I recognize in myself. It's the same thing I do when people try to dig into anything having to do with my father.

"Guess that's another thing we have in common. Dead parents and overprotective siblings." I raise my water and tap it to hers.

"That's the worst toast I've ever heard," she laughs. "How about to good dads? Everyone deserves one."

I look at my son and hope to God that's what he'll think of me one day.

~

*I*ndia

"In all seriousness, I have a question . . ." I grab Jace's empty plate and stack it on top of mine, then stand to clear the table. "What's the deal with Cohen's mom? I'm assuming she's not in the picture, but I should probably have an idea of what the situation is."

"Here." He takes the plates from my hand. "Let me get them."

Well, that answers *that*.

Jace steps into the house, ending the conversation. Guess I need to take the hint.

A firm reminder that I'm the help. *We're not friends. Got it.*

I look back at a happy little Cohen and sigh before I pick him up. "You're not going to let me sleep tonight, are you, handsome?"

His chubby hands clap my cheeks as drool drips down his chin.

"Pretty sure he just told you no." Jace's gravelly voice skims my skin before he stops and takes Cohen from me, kissing the baby's balled fist. "Wanna take a walk on the beach?"

"Why not?" I follow him along a winding trail that's away from the rocks and through the dunes. Wild grass sways in the wind on either side of the well-worn wooden before it fades away, and my toes dig into the sand beneath my feet. After that it's wide-open beach and rough blue waves crashing against the hard shore. Sandpipers skip through the surf, but no one else lingers on this stretch of beach.

Jace stops where the ocean meets the sand and stands where the waves lap at his feet. The little birds ignore his presence and stay right where they are, unafraid. Jace kisses Cohen's head as if he's pulled to him, just needing to love on his beautiful baby before he sets his sights on the ocean. "I'm not exactly proud of the man I was last year." He stares off at the horizon, and I can't keep my eyes off him. "I was out of control. It had been building for a while. A few years, at least. I was drinking too much. Partying too hard with the wrong people and the wrong stuff. It was the most freedom I'd ever had, and with everything else going on in our family, the focus was off me for a little while. So I guess I went a little crazy."

He closes his eyes, and I watch his Adam's apple work

along his throat. "I wasn't the man I should have been. The man I needed to be. The one I hope I am now."

A cool breeze off the ocean catches the loose strands of my hair as I take a step closer to Jace, quietly waiting for him to go on.

He doesn't at first. He simply stands there, slowly sinking into the wet sand until he turns my way—finally looking at me. A tortured expression haunts his eyes, one I wish I could erase for him. "I don't know who Cohen's mother is."

Of all the things Jace could have told me in that moment, I wasn't expecting that.

"I was in Canada for the draft the day he was born. His mother checked into the hospital under a fake name. She gave birth and left the next day. They never even caught her face on a camera. The only legal name she listed was mine." He cups Cohen's head and takes another step closer.

I reach out to him out of instinct but, at the last minute, run my hand down Cohen's back instead of touching Jace. The moment is raw and honest. Intimate in a way that scares me a little. "I don't even know what to say. I can't imagine a mother leaving her son behind."

"I don't even know who she was." He reaches out with a shaky hand and tugs my hair away from my face, then runs his thumb over my cheek. "And if I'm honest with myself, I'm not sure I want to know. My sister wanted to hire a PI to find her, but I told her no."

I wrap my fingers around his wrist and squeeze, knowing we're crossing an invisible line. It's a dangerous step that could lead to disaster, but for a single moment, I stand frozen. "Jace, that's awful."

"Yeah. I know. I probably should have told you that before you started, but it's not my proudest moment, and I don't want it to get out to the press." He laughs bitterly.

"You're the first person I've talked to about any of this who wasn't family."

"Thank you for telling me. I won't repeat any of it." I pull my hand back and cross my arms over my chest. "Cohen has you and your entire family, Jace. He's a lucky baby. Trust your instincts. You'll know when it's the right time to look into finding his mother."

"That's the thing. I probably should have done it already. But I didn't want to. I just wanted him. From the first fucking moment I saw him. From the moment Sawyer told me about him. I just wanted him." Thunder rumbles in the distance, and he tucks Cohen against his chest, then puts that big hand at the small of my back again. "Come on . . .We better get back in before the storm hits."

I know he's talking about the clouds, but that's not the storm I'm worried about.

There's a whole different storm brewing between the two of us.

One I think can do more damage than a little rain ever could.

## JACE

The storm never did roll in last night, but it's coming. I can smell it in the air and feel it with every rough wave while I sit in the middle of the Atlantic Ocean on my surfboard at the crack of dawn.

Mom used to take Lenny and me out here when we were little. She always said there was too much living to do to waste the day sleeping in. She wasn't wrong, considering she died before she turned forty-five. Sunrise surfing has been one of my favorite things to do when I get down here. It makes me feel closer to her.

Just me and my thoughts.

And my thoughts are fucked right now.

Thoughts like how my son will ask about his mother one day, and I won't have any answers for him unless I man up and get him the answers he deserves.

If this is the one I'm going to start with, I guess I need to call Scarlet. It's time to get her private investigator to look into Cohen's mom.

But that's not the only thought fucking with my head. My team captain thinks I'm a spoiled rich boy—too good for my teammates. Like that shouldn't make for a shit first day of training camp.

Max and I are barely on speaking terms.

And how about the fact that I've known my nanny for less than a week, and I can't stop thinking about her?

Indy is the first person I'm not related to who I've felt like I could let my guard down around. She's not at all what I was expecting when Wren told me I had to hire a nanny. She's easy to talk to. Doesn't judge. Add to that, she's the sexiest woman I've ever seen in my life—*and I've seen a whole lot of women*—and the urge to make her mine is almost irresistible.

It's not just my thoughts that are fucked.

Mom used to say there's nothing more important in life than love. Being loved and loving someone, giving them your heart, it was the ultimate form of trust. She told us when you find the one, trust your heart, hold on tight, and don't let go. You'll know it in your gut.

Trust it.

No matter what.

She was dying and trying to impart as much wisdom on us as she could at the time.

Lenny would sit there with stars in her eyes while I cringed. Show me a twelve-year-old boy who wants to hear about how important letting yourself be loved is and I'll show you ten who think it's bullshit. It was easier to act tough, like none of it mattered to me. And as far as anyone knew, it didn't.

As far as I ever let myself believe, it wouldn't.

Love was bullshit.

Until I started watching my siblings fall, one by one, starting with Lenny.

The thing is . . . they're happy in a way I've never seen them all happy before.

And for the first time, I wonder if it's worth taking the damn chance.

~

*J* put away my surfboard and grab my phone from the towel I left outside earlier, then shoot Scarlet a text.

JACE

Can you send me your PI's info when you get a chance?

The smell of bacon snakes through the open doors and draws me in later that morning. And there she is. The woman currently invading my thoughts. Somehow complicating my life but simplifying it at the same damn time. An oversized Busy Bee tee hangs off one unbelievably sexy shoulder and dwarfs her small frame. Black and white polka-dot shorts peek out beneath the tee, and I'm pretty sure I'm quickly getting addicted to her short shorts.

"Are you going to stand there and stare or fix yourself a plate?" She turns with a spatula in her hand and points it at me. "Come on. The eggs are getting cold."

"Yes, ma'am." I grab two plates and hand her one. "Thanks for breakfast."

"Don't get used to it. You hired a nanny, not a cook. But I was hungry." She drops her chin and giggles, and fuck, if that doesn't do something funny to my chest.

"Yes, ma'am." We sit at the island next to Cohen, who's kicking his bare feet in a little papasan chair that's vibrating beneath him. Today's onesie says *Daddy's Little Pucker.* I think it was a gift from Uncle Becks.

"You looked good out there this morning." She looks out the window and sighs. "I always wanted to learn to surf."

"Yeah?" I ask, liking that she was watching. "What's stopping you?"

She shrugs. "Life, I guess. Just never had the chance. Maybe someday."

My phone rings, interrupting us, and I stand when I see Scarlet's name flashing. "Hold that thought, okay? I've got to take this."

I step outside under the awning and out of the storm that's started in the last few minutes. "Hey, Scar. Thanks for getting back to me so fast. Can you send me your PI's info? I think I'm ready to find Cohen's mom."

She's quiet for a beat. Then another. "Listen, Jace . . ." She hesitates, and my stomach drops. My sister does not hesitate. She's a confident, in-your-face woman. "I knew you'd want to do this eventually, so I already have him working on it."

Fuck. I was afraid she was going to say something like that.

"You what?" I roar. "I specifically told you not to do that. *Told*, not asked, Scarlet. What the hell is wrong with you?"

"Excuse me?" she snaps back. "I'm doing what you should have done. What you were going to do."

"You're doing what *I chose* not to do." My tight grip threatens to shatter the phone as I move further away from the house, not wanting Indy and Cohen to hear this. "That was my decision to make."

"And you've made it. I just gave you a head start." Her voice holds no room for argument. It's her mom voice. She thinks she's right, but I'm like a bull focused on the blood-red flag she's waving in front of me.

"That wasn't your decision to make. This is *my* fucking life. My son's life. *My* son. Not yours. What the hell don't you guys get? You don't get to control my life. I'm a grown fucking man." Thunder cracks above my head, and the sky opens up .

"Then fucking act like it, Jace. Grown men don't bury their heads in the sand. They face the fight head-on. Hiding from it never helped anyone."

"Fuck you, Scarlet. You and Max are two fucking peas in a pod. I needed time, and instead of giving me that, you took away my choice. What would you do if someone did that to you?"

I know what she'd do.

She'd destroy anyone who dared to think they could make decisions about her life.

"Jace, just listen to me. Please . . ."

"I want his information today, Scarlet. And I swear to God, I don't want to talk to you again until Max and you stop trying to control my life. You both already control the Kingston empire. Let that be enough, because I'm done being controlled." I end the call, drop my hand, then raise it, readying to throw it like a baseball on opening day.

"Jace . . ." Indy soft voice calls, but I don't turn around.

Can't.

"Jace." Her voice pulls me back from the edge before I feel her warm palm between my wet shoulder blades. She doesn't say anything else. Doesn't ask if I'm okay. I guess it's pretty obvious I'm not.

Neither of us move.

It's like she's breathing with me, willing me to calm down.

But that's impossible, the way her touch burns my fucking skin.

"I'm so goddamned tired of everyone else deciding what I need to do and who I need to be. I'm done playing by their rules." My breathing slows as I gain control. The warm rain covers us before I shove my phone into my pocket and turn to face her.

She's soaked to the bone. Her hair is plastered to her face, and her white shirt is drenched and molded to her incredible tits. My palms itch to touch her skin, to cover every fucking delectable inch of it with my mouth. My tongue. To fuck her until she's screaming my name.

I gather her face in my hands and watch the gold flecks dance with desire in her whiskey eyes.

She feels it too.

"Do you want me to kiss you, India?" I growl.

She flutters her soaked lashes, licks her wet lips, then puts her palms flat against my bare chest. "Not now. Not like this, when you're furious with your sister. I moved my life into your house two days ago, Jace. I went against my grandfather and my brother and took this job. I didn't do it so I could sleep with you and have to quit in the morning."

She takes a step back. "I'm no one's mistake, Jace Kingston. So, if you want to kiss me, you better be sure. And you better be doing it because you can't imagine not kissing me. Not touching me. Don't you dare do it because you're mad at someone else."

I watch her take another tentative step back, then another before she turns around and runs into the house.

Fuck.

~

*I*ndia

Oh. My. God.

What the hell just happened?

Cohen is sound asleep in his little papasan chair, so I grab the whole damn chair and carry it up to my room carefully. So fucking carefully.

*Little man, you don't know me that well yet. But I'm freaking begging you not to wake up right now.*

Thankfully, he stays asleep, and once my door is shut and

locked for good measure, I grab my phone. This is going to take Sophie and Harper.

I call Sophie first, then add Harper into the FaceTime. "Guys . . . I need your help," I whisper.

"Uh, Indy . . . ?" Harper's eyes narrow. "Why are you sitting next to a toilet?"

"Because I don't want Jace to hear me, and this room is further away from the door," I tell her, hearing how insane that must sound.

Sophie's eyes light up. "Ohh. What don't you want the hockey hottie to hear?"

"Oh, God. Did you sleep with him already?" Harper walks down a crowded hall. "Not that I'd blame you. Jace Kingston is—"

"Stop. I don't want to hear what you think he is." I also don't want to analyze why hearing her talk about him like that makes me irrationally angry. "I've worked for the man for three freaking days, and I know exactly what he is. Trust me. He's hard to read and even harder to resist. He's unbelievably gorgeous. His hands are huge and warm, and his smile . . . Oh God," I groan. "I think his smile could incinerate my panties. Oh. *Oh.* Oh . . . and his laugh. Holy shit when this man laughs, it's so freaking hot," I ramble. "And the way he loves Cohen melts my freaking heart already. After three days."

"She fucked him," Sophie squeals.

"I didn't. But I did just run away from him because he was going to kiss me. I can't believe the way I talked to him either. I'm probably going to get fired." I cringe, thinking about what I'm going to tell Gramps and Atlas.

"He can't fire you for not fucking him, Indy." Harper shuts a door behind her and slides down onto the floor.

"Where are you, Harps?" Sophie asks.

"I'm in a dressing room. I was picking up new lingerie for

a client, and I don't want everyone in the shop to hear me talking." Of course, she's in public.

Harper tsks. "Oh please. Like I haven't done worse things than this in public."

Somebody shoot me now.

"What am I going to do, guys?" I'm so screwed.

Harper adjusts the phone, then gets serious. "Did you want to kiss him?"

"Have you seen him? Of course, she wanted to kiss him, Harps." Sophie's not wrong.

"I think I did want him to kiss me," I admit, as scared of the words I'm saying as I am of the truth behind them.

The two of them laugh in unison.

"Don't laugh. It's not funny, guys. This is my life. I signed a one-year contract. I can't screw my boss."

"Oh yes you can, India Monroe. Virgin or not, you can 100 percent screw your boss. But you're getting too far ahead of yourself right now, and you've skipped all the good stuff that happens before you screw him," Sophie lectures.

Harper agrees, "When was the last time you let a guy in, Indy? It was before you moved to Kroydon Hills, right? So I know it was before your surgery. Maybe you should try letting this one in before you decide to give up the cookie."

"Oh my God, Harper. Do not call it *the cookie*. That's just icky," I laugh.

"Oh, babe. Just wait till he *eats* your cookie. Trust me. If they do it right, there ain't a damn thing icky about it." Harper's smile grows while Sophie and I laugh at her.

"Seriously, I can't go there because I can't lose this job. What if it doesn't work out? What do I do then?" My stomach rolls at the thought of being broke and living with Gramps again. "And can I really date my boss while he's paying me to do a job? Doesn't that make me a hooker?"

It's Sophie's turn to give me a serious face now. "He's

paying you to be a nanny, not his girlfriend. You're both adults, Indy. If it doesn't work out, you finish your contract, pay off your student loans, and stash everything else in your savings for your medical expenses. With what he's paying you, you'll be set while you look for a new job. I think you're making a bigger deal out of this than it needs to be."

"I agree with Sophie. You're both adults. I say go for it." Someone knocks on the door to the dressing room Harper is hiding in. "Shit, guys. I gotta go. Indy . . . make sure he licks the cookie before you give it away. Bye, bitches." She disconnects, and I palm my face.

"Hey, Indy . . ." Sophie says a little too sweetly.

"Yeah?"

"You might want to fix your hair and put on a shirt I can't see through before you talk to him again. Your tits are fantastic, but I can see the color of your nipples through your wet shirt."

I adjust the phone and glare at my best friend.

"Love you." She blows me a kiss.

"Love you too." I end the call, more confused than I was before.

# INDIA

*C*ohen and I stay cocooned in my room for the next hour, while he sleeps and I silently freak out. Well, that and change my clothes. *Twice.* Because now, I'm paranoid. *Thank you very much, Sophie.* By the time he wakes up, needing a diaper and a bottle, there's a lull in the storm outside. But as I open the bedroom door, the one inside rages on.

At least, for me it does.

Cohen cries when we make our way downstairs. I've learned quickly this little man has *hanger* issues that make Harper's look like a walk in the park. When he wants to eat, he wants it right then and there. In the time it takes for me to change him, clean him up, because—*hello,* blowout—and get to the kitchen, he's gone from whimpers to full-on fit.

I pop a bottle in the warmer and sway with him in my arms, attempting to calm him until the warmer beeps, and I gratefully grab the damn bottle. "Shh . . . handsome man. It's okay."

I run the bottle over his lips after testing the temperature, and as soon as that nipple hits those tiny lips, he's a happy camper again. Crisis avoided. Thank goodness.

The headache that started at the back of my skull during the call to Harper and Sophie has been steadily building, so a happy Cohen is way easier to deal with right now. We walk into the den, and I stop when I see Jace standing there. A faded Revolution t-shirt is stretched over his broad chest. It's the kind of shirt that's so old, the material is practically see-through. His big hands are shoved in the pocket of ripped-up old jeans, and the man is barefoot.

Confident and mouth-wateringly sexy in his skin.

"Can I hold him?" he asks hesitantly, and I immediately feel like an asshole.

"Of course." I cross the room, stopping in front of him, and place Cohen in his arms and the burp cloth on his shoulder. "Sorry. I shouldn't have put him in my room. I didn't think—"

"Don't," he cuts me off. "You have nothing to be sorry for, Indy. That's all me." Jace moves to the windows and stares out at the gloomy day. "I shouldn't have done that earlier. It wasn't fair to you."

My heart sinks at his regret, and frustration grows with my sinking heart.

My feet stay firmly planted where they are—across from my gorgeous boss. I may be a walking, talking hypocrite, but at least I'm not giving mixed signals. "I shouldn't have said what I did either."

Jace pulls the bottle from Cohen's mouth and moves him to his shoulder to burp him, then turns to face me. Confidence suddenly oozes off him again, giving me another round of whiplash. "You weren't wrong, Indy. Not about any of it."

He takes a few steps my way, and when Cohen burps, he lays him back in the crook of his arm for the rest of his bottle. I don't think he gives himself enough credit for how good he is with his son. "The thing is, I wanted to kiss you earlier. I wanted to kiss you yesterday. And I wanted to kiss you the day we met, six months ago."

By the time he stops talking, we're standing toe-to-toe, and I have to look up at him just to see his face. "But I'm not sorry I want to kiss you, Indy. I'm sorry I put you in an uncomfortable position. I'm sorry I did it when my emotions were running high. I'm sorry you thought it was just a reaction to a shitty phone call. And I'm fucking sorry I didn't do it before you worked for me. But I'm sure as hell not gonna lie and say I don't want to kiss you."

"Oh," is all I manage to say as my heart races, and my smart watch vibrates against my wrist, alerting me to the accelerated rate. As if I could have missed it.

"Here's the thing . . ." He bends his knees slightly to look me in the eyes, and I think one of those old-fashioned fainting fans would come in handy right about now.

"I want to do a lot more than kiss you." Jace's voice drops to a sexy, commanding, baritone. "I want to get to know you. I want to see if this thing running hot between us is what I think it could be, because I haven't stopped thinking about you since seeing you again last week. But I need you to understand a few things first."

I think I stop breathing, wondering where exactly he's going with this.

"I'm a package deal. I know you're here, and you're taking care of Cohen now. But if we do this, he's always going to be part of it. Part of me. Part of us. Which is not exactly normal for people our age. But it's my life." He blows out a frustrated breath. "My very public life. That's the other thing. I want to keep my life as private as I can. It's for him and me, and if you're willing to take a chance on me, maybe for you too. It's a fucking balancing act I haven't perfected yet."

"Jace . . . I appreciate you laying it all out there like this, but this,"—I motion between us— "this scares the shit out of me. I just got this job, and like I told you before, I need it. What are we supposed to do if we decide to give this a try and it doesn't work out?"

He looks down at me and grins. "Oh, pretty girl, but what if it does?"

I open my mouth to answer him, but nothing comes out.

"Want to go grab lunch? There's this little place at the wharf. We've been going there for years. No one will bother us." Cohen sucks the last drops of his bottle and whines. "Come to lunch with us, Indy."

"Using Cohen is cheating, Kingston," I tease because I don't know what else to say.

"Gotta use all my tricks. And the little man is the ace up my sleeve. Come on. Let's get out of the house before it pours again."

I'm pretty sure I'm incapable of telling this man no.

I'm even less sure I care.

~

*J*ace

We sit on the covered deck of the old restaurant and watch the boats come and go as fat raindrops hit the bay all around us.

Cohen's chilling in his seat next to me as Indy nervously works the straw wrapper around her fingers.

I open my straw, pull the wrapper down a little, and blow it at her to ease the tension.

When she finally gives me her golden eyes, I relax a little. "You know, I didn't even ask if you were seeing someone." I feel bad for the poor guy if she is because he's got no chance.

Indy gently shakes her head. "No. Not seeing anyone." She

releases a sad, sarcastic laugh, which immediately sets me on edge, and the need to dig deeper surfaces.

"Sounds like there's a story there, pretty girl." Her eyes drop to the table, and she shakes her head, but a small smile tugs at her lips, so I'll take it as a win. "Wanna tell me about him . . . or her?" I push.

"Jace," she sighs. "There is no him or her. There's no big story to tell. I moved in with Gramps my senior year in high school, right after my mom died, and I guess I kept to myself after that. Then I started college and was determined to graduate in three and a half years. That didn't leave a ton of time for dating." She twists her hair up and scrunches a rubber band around it nervously. "My life is boring, and that's how I like it."

"Come on," I push harder, wanting to know more and not buying that no guy ever tried to date Indy. "No dates at all?"

She cocks her head to the side, considering the question. "I didn't say that. I said I never got into a relationship. Not since high school."

"What happened in high school?" I want to know everything about her. What makes her tick. What makes her hide.

"Has anyone ever told you you're like a dog with a bone?" she questions as she sips her sweet tea.

"I may have been called a dog once or twice." I rest my elbows on the table and lean in toward her. "Has anyone ever told you it's not nice to answer a question with a question?"

"Touché, Jace Kingston. Fine." She mirrors my position. "Another round of a question for a question?"

"Sure." I lean back as a server places our plates in front of us and coos at Cohen before walking away. "You first. Tell me about your high-school boyfriend."

Indy takes a bite of her lobster roll and moans. "Oh, wow. This is so good." She holds it up. "Do you want a taste?"

More than you know, pretty girl.

I lean across the table, grip her wrist, and take a bite of the buttery sandwich, my eyes locked on hers while I do it. "That's good," I keep my eyes trained on hers when I wrap my lips around her thumb and suck off the sauce. Her pupils dilate, and I let go. "Now spill."

She stalls, taking a sip of her iced tea, before answering me. "Fine. Yes, I had a high-school boyfriend. He was one of Atlas's teammates, which had the added bonus of pissing off my brother. I thought it was more serious than he did, though, and when things got tough, he bailed. End of story. We moved a year later."

She's not telling me everything, but I don't push harder.

Not yet.

She'll tell me when she's ready.

"How about you? When was your last relationship?"

"I think I was twelve . . . Maybe thirteen. April Deegan. She was the first girl in class to not wear shorts under her uniform skirt, and when she bent over, you could see her panties. It was love at first sight." I chuckle as I remember the first time I jerked off to the tiny bit of ass cheek I caught when she bent over in science class. Seventh grade, and that girl already knew how to get a guy's attention.

Indy's chest bounces with silent laughter. "Wow. Sounds like true love. How long did you and April date?"

"Let's see . . ." I think back to that time in my life. The innocent days before Mom died, life changed, and so did I. "I think she dumped me at a party, after a less than memorable time spent in the closet playing "Seven Minutes in Heaven." She was dating Bobby Moriarty the following week."

"No serious relationships since then?"

"Nope. Never really saw a need in high school or college. I dated girls. We hooked up. But never anything serious. I was always too busy with hockey, and I never met anyone who made me want more." I hear myself, and maybe I hear a little bit of what my sisters have been telling me for years about living a shallow life, and I don't like it.

"What changed?" she counters.

"That's easy," I steal a fry from her plate. "You."

"How can you say that? You don't even know me, Jace."

"Haven't you ever felt something so strongly, you were sure of it right away? That you just knew in your gut it was the right thing? That it was worth fighting for?" I lean back as a seagull swoops down next to us and grabs a fry from the floor before flying away. "I've got this feeling, Indy. And I know it sounds crazy, but crazy doesn't scare me."

"Fine. Tell me about your family." The rain picks up again outside, playing a relaxing song against the bay, and Indy eases back in her chair, waiting for my answer.

"Don't think I missed that this is your second question. You owe me one." She runs her teeth over her lip, and I get lost in the idea of doing the same damn thing for a hot fucking minute before clearing my head. "My family. Let's see. That's a bit of a loaded question. I'm the second youngest of nine. I was the youngest until my sister Madeline was born six years ago. So, I'm pretty used to being the baby of the family. Four brothers, four sisters, some more over-bearing than others. Max and Scarlet are the oldest, and I'm not on great terms with either one of them right now."

"Why not?" She takes another bite of her sandwich, then licks the sauce from her lips, and *fuck*, she's got to be doing that on purpose.

"Max bought the Revolution two years ago. My whole goal in life has been to play pro hockey, and until then, I wanted to play for the Revolution. They've been my favorite team my whole life. But I never wanted to play for my family. I wanted to go somewhere I could prove myself without the Kingston name attached to it. I asked him not to draft me, but he did it anyway." I get angry just thinking about it.

"Scarlet and he like to think they know what's best for every-one. But sometimes you need to do things on your own terms. I'm at that point, and I've drawn a line in the sand. They've got to back off."

"It sounds like they love you."

"They do. And as far as they're concerned, they're just trying to take care of their family. But I'm not their kid or their responsibility. And I need them to back off."

Cohen spits his binky out and whines, so I take him out of his seat and hold him as he stares at me, smiling, and my anger melts away.

"Life's too short to be mad at the people you love, Jace. But I think you know that."

Our waitress stops back at the table. "Can I get you guys anything else today?"

Indy shakes her head, and I pull a few twenties out of my wallet. "No thanks. I think we're good."

The waitress cashes out my bill next to us as Cohen starts to fuss. Indy stands and grabs the diaper bag, then takes him from me. "How about I go change the little man before we go home?"

"Thanks." The word catches in my throat as I watch her walk away with the most important thing in my life until our waitress clears her throat.

"Your family is beautiful," she tells me, and I don't bother correcting her.

They sure are.

# JACE

*W*hen we get back to the house, I know what I have to do. "Are you okay with Cohen while I make a call?"

"Of course," Indy smiles, and I have to remind myself I can't kiss her yet.

I excuse myself into the office and shut the door behind me, then pull up the information Scarlet sent me earlier for her private investigator. It rings twice before a voice answers, "Hastings."

"This is Jace Kingston. My sister Scarlet gave me your name and number. I believe you've been looking into my son's mother for her."

"Ahh . . . Mr. Kingston. I hoped I'd be hearing from you. As I told your sister earlier, I believe I'm onto something and hope to have more information for you shortly."

My heart drops into my stomach.

"Thank you," I manage to tell him before giving him my contact information and ending the call, hoping I'm not about to open Pandora's box.

When I walk out of the room, it's with a clearer mind than I've had in months.

I guess sometimes you really do have to get away from everything to get perspective on anything. I need answers for Cohen when he asks the questions that'll inevitably come one day. I also need his biological mother to legally sign over her parental rights while I'm at it. Cohen's *my* son. I might be grateful this mystery woman gave him to me, but I have absolutely no intention of sharing him with her.

I don't share. *Anyone.*

When I come out of the office, I catch sight of Indy standing in front of the floor-to-ceiling windows as the lightning crashes in the distance. She's breathtakingly gorgeous. And in jean shorts and a cropped cream sweater, she's teasing just enough skin to make a man's mouth water with want.

*Yeah . . . perspective.*

I needed a little.

I step up behind her and trail my finger along the soft skin of her neck. "Is Cohen sleeping?"

Indy shivers and stutters out a "Y-yes."

"So, whose turn did we leave off on?" We've been playing Twenty Questions for days. No better way to get to know someone than to actually listen to them. And I've made it my mission to find out everything there is to know about this woman.

"Let's see . . ." She turns to face me and presses a shaky palm to my chest. "I'm pretty sure you'd just admitted that Scarlet is your scariest sibling. Which would make it your turn."

I cover her hand with mine and think about it for a minute. "Why kindergarten?"

"That's an easy one." She relaxes against me. "I want to get them when they're still young enough to love school. I want to be one of their first memories of their education. I want them to love it from the start."

"Spoken like a true teacher." I lean my forehead against hers. "I'm selfishly glad Cohen and I got you this year, but you'll make an incredible teacher, Indy."

"How would you know?" she asks on a whisper.

"Because I already feel like I've known you forever. Like this was supposed to happen the first time we met, and we got cheated. Because I feel like you're supposed to be mine."

She doesn't say anything.

Instead, her big, Bambi-like golden eyes blink slowly.

Eyelashes flutter against her cheeks as she presses a hand to her mouth and pulls away.

"Indy . . ."

"You can't mean those words, Jace." Her voice trembles as I close the distance between us, desperate to make her mine.

"Why not, pretty girl? Haven't you ever been absolutely sure of something? Followed your gut instinct?" I settle my hands on her hips, my fingers rubbing the soft skin under her thin sweater. "Because I like trusting my instincts. When I ignore them is when I tend to fuck everything up."

She shakes her head. "You don't know me, Jace."

My thumbs rub circles on her bare skin, eliciting a shiver from this beautiful woman in front of me. "Not everything. No. But I think I do know *you*."

~

*I*ndia

I pull back and look up at his blue eyes. His pupils are dilated and dark. "I'm trying to be good here, Indy. Trying to give you the time and space you need. But fuck, baby . . ." He drags out the word as his heart speeds up under my palm. "You're making it so damn hard."

He presses a kiss against the side of my neck, his lips firm and warm as a litany of sensations explode against my skin. One big hand cups the nape of my neck as the other circles my waist and presses against the small of my back, holding me to him until every soft curve of my body is pressed against every hard inch of his. His lips glide along my bare skin over my shoulder, and *oh God*, his rough tongue trails a path that lights up each of my nerve endings.

My fingers dig into his soft tee, gripping desperately when his firm lips finally meet mine, the connection teetering between too much and not nearly enough. Delicious and dangerous and so promising. The firm muscles of his chest bunch under my grip, and without thought, I let go and run my hands under his shirt. Up his sides and over his ribs. His skin is warm and soft, covering tight stacks of muscles that are firm under my fingertips.

Jace groans as my nails dig into his skin, and his insanely hard dick presses against my stomach.

I gasp as he licks into my mouth.

This kiss is slow and sensuous, teasing a promise of more to come.

"Jace . . ." I don't know what I'm trying to say or what I need, but it's more than this. "I need—"

His hand slides down from my back and over the curve of my ass. His heat sears my skin through my shorts, those rough fingers teasing and tempting. "Tell me what you need, Indy. Give me your words, and I'll give you everything."

I bunch his shirt up and over his chest, then drop it to the ground and drag my nails along the broad muscles of his chest. Jace sucks in a breath when I skim over one tight nipple, then the other. "What if I told you I don't know what I need?"

A hand wraps gently around my throat, and his thumb presses over my thrumming pulse. He pulls his head back, and it's as if the depths of his steely-blue eyes pull me down to the bottom of a stormy ocean, drowning me in its depths.

"What are you telling me, Indy?" His voice is strained and strangled. But he knows. He didn't before now, but that one sentence gave him everything I couldn't say.

I kiss the edge of his jaw as my pulse speeds up. Not scared. *No.* Jace Kingston makes me feel safe in a way I'm not sure I've ever felt before. I rub my body against his, knowing I need to tell him. Knowing this . . . *us* . . . This is all leading to something bigger than I could have ever anticipated when I took this job.

I take a step back and raise my hand, stopping him when he reaches for me.

His eyes hold me captive when I take a deep breath and with shaking hands, lift my shirt over my head and drop it to the ground.

His gaze stays locked on mine. "Jace . . . I've never done this before."

I take a hesitant step back into his space and lift his hand to my lips, then place it over the top of my sternum, touching the top of my scar. I hold it there, willing my racing, broken heart to slow down. "I had heart surgery when I was sixteen."

"Indy—" His voice strains.

I cover his lips with my fingers. "Just let me get this out first. Please," I plead. "I had a boyfriend before then, but not after. Having a girlfriend with staples holding her chest together isn't sexy, and having one with a fresh scar, or a healing scar, isn't much better. I needed the surgery so I could live. It might have meant that my chances at a boyfriend . . . my chances at any kind of sexual experience became nonexistent. But it meant that I'd have a chance at life."

Jace's fingers trace the slightly puckered skin in the valley between my breasts reverently. His eyes now watching what he's doing, no longer locked on mine. "Are you okay now?" He looks up and cradles my face with the hand not running over my scar. "Does it hurt? Do you need anything?" Agony laces each of his words. "Is there anything I should know? Anything we should look out for? What do we need to do?"

His usually strong voice is weak and heartbreaking, and yet it gives me hope.

I shake my head gently. "No. There's nothing you need to know or look out for. I take a cocktail of prescriptions daily and see my cardiologist quarterly. I don't typically share this part of me with anyone else." I turn my head slightly and kiss his palm. "I guess I just needed you to know the truth before . . ." I choke off the rest of my words and look away, suddenly unsure and not wanting to make a fool of myself.

Jace lifts my face to his. "You are beautiful, India Monroe, and that scar should be fucking worshipped if that's the reason you're standing here in front of me today." He presses his lips against my skin, taking my breath away. "But I don't think your scar is the reason you've never done this before, Indy." He lifts me from my feet and kisses me slowly. Deeply. With so much need it warms me from the inside out, then carries me up the stairs.

"Jace . . . what are you doing?" I cling to him.

"You're mine, pretty girl. And I'm the only man who'll ever touch your skin." He makes his way through the house, then takes the stairs two at a time. "I want you spread out on a bed the first time I taste your sweet cunt. I want to take my time and worship every inch of your body until you're begging me to let you come."

A violent shiver racks my body as I cling to him, wanting everything he's willing to give.

When we get to his bedroom, he lays me gently down on his bed. The look in his eyes is greedy and possessive and so heavy, I feel it everywhere.

He presses his lips against my scar, then trails his mouth down, kissing me through the lace of my bra. My nipples press against the fabric, tight little peaks straining, desperate to be touched,. I suck in a breath when he pulls my breast into his mouth, his teeth tugging on my nipple and his other hand kneading my breast. The rough pad of his thumb brushes over me before he drags his warm, wet mouth down my body.

Groaning, his tongue swirls a circle around my belly button and my abs shake as I try to control my breathing, while both Jace's hands grip my hips, holding them in place.

"Jace . . . please."

"Oh, don't you worry, darlin'." His fingers pop open the buttons of my shorts one at a time. The soft sound seems to be the only thing louder than my wildly beating heart.

Slowly, he tugs my shorts down, kissing each of my hip bones, then running his nose along the black lace of my panties, and my body jerks in response.

"Don't worry, I'm going to give you everything you need, baby."

My back arches off the bed as he inhales, then drags his tongue along my sex over the lace. The friction flames the fire already building inside me.

"Do you want me to taste you, Indy?" When I don't answer right away, he misreads my silence for hesitance. "Your pace, pretty girl. You say stop, and we stop."

"Please don't stop." My hands dig into Jace's sandy-blond hair, and my ability to think vanishes, taking any self-preservation with it, when he snaps the side of my panties, tearing them from my body, and buries his face in my drenched sex.

One arm slides under my hips, lifting me to his mouth, and he sucks my clit between his lips, then licks again. His warm mouth against my bare lips drives me insane.

So sensitive. So good. So different from when I get myself off.

It's all so much.

Too much.

I didn't know . . .

Couldn't know what the feel of his warm mouth kissing my pussy would do to me.

How his teeth grazing my clit would make me tremble.

And oh God, when his tongue spears my pussy, I think I could come from that alone. But then he plunges a finger inside me . . . And tongues my clit over and over, adding another finger, stretching me .

The rough intrusion feels so tight . . . so good, I can't help but buck my hips shamelessly.

I tug on Jace's hair, whimpering as my body grows tense and impossibly tight until I'm a balloon stretched so tautly, any movement will make me pop.

I fuck Jace's face as he growls against my sex, and *God*, it's so fucking sexy.

He adds a third finger, working me into oblivion, and the balloon pops. I come suddenly, without warning. Explosive. Convulsing around his fingers while he licks me through my orgasm.

Once he wrings every last tremor from my body and I'm positive I'll never be the same, he leans over me, such a fucking sight to see. Bare chest and broad shoulders, sculpted abs, and a perfect V disappearing into his jeans. He runs his wet finger over my lips, my juices dripping over my skin until I dart my tongue out and lick them clean.

I reach up and wrap an arm around his shoulders, then cover his mouth with mine, tasting myself on his lips. Licking and sucking as he groans.

"Fucking incredible, Indy. You're fucking perfect."

One hand snakes down his body, and I unsnap the top button of his jeans and slide my hand inside.

"Baby, no." He rolls to the side and pulls me to his chest. "Tonight was for you."

I drag my hand over his heart. "Why can't tonight be for both of us?" I pout, wanting to give him what he just gave me.

He runs his hand through my hair. "Because I'm not sure I can be gentle right now."

"Who says I want you to be gentle?" I tug on his jeans until he stands, looking down over me, his gaze raw and heavy.

"Are you sure, Indy?" He stands before me, so strong and powerful and somehow still unbelievably willing to take it at my pace. A promise of more in his eyes.

A promise I'm all too ready for.

I lift to my knees and press my lips to his. "God, yes. Please, Jace," I beg, tired of worrying and waiting.

He reaches into the nightstand and pulls out a foil packet without breaking our contact, then shucks out of his jeans and boxers.

"Fuck me," I plead, wanting to feel his weight on me.

He places my trembling hand over his and guides me as I roll the condom down the length of his cock. It's so big and hard and begging for attention. When I run my tongue along the base of his dick, wanton with need, he lets out a guttural groan and lowers us to the bed.

He runs his hand along my temple, gently brushing my hair from my face and covering my mouth with his as he hitches my leg over his hip. "Breathe, Indy," he whispers against my lips, raw and unguarded as he pushes inside me with a sexy groan, holding back, afraid to hurt me.

The invasion is quick, stretching me so tightly, my breath catches, and pain sparks hot in my chest in the silence of the room.

A guttural cry tears from my throat, and my body splits in two. I gasp and wrap both legs around Jace's hips, toes pointing and muscles tightening as I cling to him. He holds himself above me, perfectly still, the lines of his face rigid and firm. "Jace . . . move."

His eyes light up with an unmistakable need that makes me feel so utterly feminine. Desired and beautiful in a way I've never felt before.

He takes my mouth in his, his tongue dancing with mine as he pulls himself back, then slowly fucks into me. Pleasure mixes with pain. "Jesus, Indy. You're so tight. You feel so fucking good."

His muscles tighten beneath my hands as I explore every inch of his magnificent body.

My breath hitches, and he thrusts again. Harder. "You were made for me, Indy. Mine." His hips snap against me. "Only mine. Only ever mine."

He leans up on his knees, hands gripping my hips, and drags his cock almost completely out. "Look at us, baby."

I watch the almost obscene way his cock disappears inside me.

Blood is smeared on my thighs, glinting on the condom.

I lift up and wrap my arms around his neck, digging my nails into his back. "I fucking love it."

"Tell me how it feels. Tell me what you want," he growls above me, and my pulse skyrockets.

He lays me back, our fingers laced, and presses me into the mattress, then lifts his chest from mine, waiting for his answer.

"I . . . I feel tight." He rolls his hips against mine, dragging his cock along my hypersensitive walls. "And wet." Another snap of his hips, and the pain melts away as pleasure engulfs me. "And so fucking full . . ."

Jace's eyes glaze over as he thrusts into me again and

again. I lift my hips to meet his, and a warm shiver washes over my body from the new contact. His cock drags against a sensitive spot inside me that's never been touched before. Not even by my favorite vibrator.

"Are you going to give me what I want, baby?" His hot mouth takes mine in a desperate kiss, and I shake beneath him. "Come with my name on your lips," he demands.

The weight of his hips against mine.

Our hands joined and buried in the mattress.

Jace's chest brushing over me.

It's all too much.

This orgasm is a slow build.

A warm wave dragging me under. Stealing my breath and my thoughts and all my senses until it's just him and me and nothing else exists but us. I come, gasping and clawing and chanting his name. And when he follows me over the edge, it's with my name on his lips like a sacred promise that should scare me, but somehow doesn't, because I'm right there with him.

# INDIA

"So . . ." He traces the ridges of my spine with the tips of his finger until I'm practically purring beneath his touch. "Do you want to go to a Kings game with us tomorrow?"

"Kings?" I lift my heavy head and look at Jace in the darkness of the room we haven't left for hours. *Hours.* "Like the football team?"

Jace smiles, both dimples popping deep in his cheeks. "Yes, pretty girl. Football. My family has a private box to watch the game, and it's all decked out for the kids. It's kind of a tradition for us all to go to the first game of the season. We've done it pretty much our entire lives. My sister Lenny's husband is the team's defensive end and Hudson's wife's brother is the center. So now, we actually have family on the field. It's pretty cool."

"Then we better not miss it." I roll over and drop my head to his chest, pressing my lips to his strong pec.

What could go wrong?

*W*e make it to the stadium the next night, just before the start of the game, and when we step inside, my heart rate speeds from anxious energy. There's a whole lot of people in this room. "This is just your family?"

"Yeah." He looks around before anyone notices we're here, one hand around my waist and the other holding Cohen. "Looks like everyone else is already here."

His family is huge.

Brothers, sisters, and spouses are spread throughout the large space, laughing and talking as waiters set up a buffet along one wall, while kids decked out in black and gold Kings football jerseys run wild.

Jace unbuckles Cohen from his car seat and drops a kiss on my lips.

"Low-key," I remind him, not wanting his siblings to get the wrong idea the first time they meet me.

*Hi. I'm the poor nanny who's already sleeping with her rich boss.*

This is such a bad idea.

Wren is the first to notice us and quickly makes a beeline straight for Cohen.

"Come here, my baby," she coos as she steals him right out of Jace's arms. "Your daddy thinks it's okay to move out and then take you away from me for a week." She nuzzles her nose in Cohen's neck and breathes in his sweet baby scent.

I don't blame her.

There's something so calming about holding the little man. "I missed you, baby boy."

Her loving demeanor changes, however, when she turns her eyes on Jace. "Did I not let you live with us for months?" she asks, clearly unhappy with him. "Hmm? I can't hear you."

Jace nods like a little boy. "Yes, Wren."

"Who helped you when you brought Cohen home from the hospital and you and your idiot brother had no idea how to take care of a baby?" She kisses Cohen again, and Jace shrinks back a little while trying to hide his smile.

"Hey . . ." Sawyer joins us, wrapping an arm around his wife. "You're married to that idiot brother. Be nice."

"Potato. Po-tah-to." She shrugs and steps away, linking her arm through mine. "Come on, Indy. Let me introduce you to the family."

"She was at the beach too," Jace pleads.

"Hey." I point my finger at him, smiling. "Don't throw me under the bus. It was your idea."

I don't look back as I'm drug across the room, sidestepping toddler boys and a little girl, all decked out in Beneventi jerseys, and a baby girl in a glittery pink-and-black Dixon jersey with a pink tutu over black leggings and a teeny-tiny blonde ponytail high on her head.

I like that one's style.

Wren stops at a high-top table in front of the floor-to-ceiling glass windows, giving us a perfect view of a sold-out Kings Stadium.

Atlas would love this.

"So . . ." Wren's eyes narrow on me as she sways with Cohen in her arms. "How are you settling in?"

Before I can answer, two women join us in the corner of the box. The shorter of the two I've known for a few years. She owns Sweet Temptations where Sophie works. "Hi, Amelia."

Jace's sister Amelia's smile is as warm and welcoming as always when she hugs me. "It's so good to see you, Indy. How are you?"

"Good, thanks," I answer when the other woman gives me a slightly more predatory smile that looks so much like her brother's, it's a little unsettling.

She's taller than Amelia and wearing a Beneventi jersey that stretches over a pregnant belly. "Hi. I'm Lenny, Jace's older sister."

"Nice to meet you, Lenny." I offer her my hand. "I'm Indy. And wow . . ." I look from Cohen to her. "Cohen looks just like you."

"Ohh. I like her," she says to her sister. "We're going to keep this one."

Jace comes up behind me and wraps an arm around my shoulder, tugging me possessively back to his chest. "Yes. We are."

So much for low-key.

Three sets of eyes grow wide as the room quiets, and I pray for a hole to open up that I can crawl into.

"Jace," Amelia barks. "What did we talk about?"

I don't like the sound of that and turn toward my boss slash new boyfriend and stare. "Yeah, Jace. What *did* you talk about?"

He kisses the top of my head, like that's going to smooth this over. "It's not like that."

Why am I not surprised that Jace Kingston has no problem with PDA?

Amelia shakes her head and looks between the two of us. "Oh my . . ." She sips her wine when the ridiculous number of adults in the room suddenly swarm like sharks circling their next victim, and I'm the blood in the water.

I suddenly feel like the odds are stacked against me.

"Damn, brother." A big blond man punches Jace in the shoulder. You couldn't have held out for another week?"

Umm . . . What?

Amelia's husband, Sam, walks over with a shit-eating grin. This guy could make grown men pee their pants, and I think he might have once or twice at The Bee, but he's always been sweet to me. "Pay up, assholes. I told you he wouldn't last a week." He flashes me a smile. "Hey, Indy."

"Hi, Sam." Amelia Beneventi is a lucky, *lucky* woman.

"She was always going to be perfect for him," Sam adds, and I blush a furious red.

The group grumbles as everyone starts smacking Sam's hand with twenty-dollar bills.

"You guys are assholes," Jace groans while his siblings laugh at him. "I didn't . . . We . . ." He looks at me, then back at them. "We just . . ." His fingers dig into my hip protectively as he stumbles over his words.

"Wait a second," I call out, and over a dozen sets of eyes turn my way. "Did you guys bet on whether we'd have sex?"

Maybe I should have filtered myself before I asked a room full of people I don't know about whether they'd bet on my previously nonexistent sex life. But what the hell?

As I say the words, the laughter starts, and Amelia smacks Jace's chest. "I told you not to bang the nanny, you shit."

I look around at the group, then take the money out of Sam's hand and smile.

*Hey, that's a lot of twenties.*

"He didn't *bang* the nanny," I announce, then pocket the money, not feeling at all bad. Banging the nanny implies there's nothing else going on between us. And Jace Kingston made it crystal clear to me we're so much more than that. So maybe I fib . . . just a little. "He's been a perfect gentleman. And since Jace and I are the only ones who will know what goes on behind closed doors, I'm pretty sure I just won the bet." I turn toward Wren and take Cohen from her. "I think it's time for his bottle."

I walk away and hear a snicker behind me, followed by what I *think* is Lenny's voice saying, "And that, folks, is a mic-drop moment. You better lock that one down, little brother."

"Pretty sure he already did, Len," Becket tells her.

"If you idiots don't fuck it up for me," Jace mutters.

~

 'm introduced to everyone throughout the evening after the little bet snafu at the start.

Jace's family is loud and obnoxious. They have zero filter, and they're absolutely awesome. At least until Scarlet sits down across from me during the fourth quarter. "How mad is he?" she asks, like I'm supposed to know what she's talking about.

Which I probably do.

But I'm not about to tell her that.

I've watched Jace avoid her and his oldest brother, Max, all night. It's pretty obvious he's not ready to talk to them yet.

"I don't know what you're talking about," I tell her as I sip a bottle of water.

"Don't play coy with me, India. I've been doing it longer. And according to my baby brother, you're going to be around for a while as more than Cohen's nanny. So we might as well be friends."

"Listen. I don't know you. I only know what Jace has told me and what I've overheard. It isn't my place to have this conversation."

Scarlet drags her eyes over me, settling on Cohen. "Here's the thing. If my brother has brought you here tonight, it tells me a few things. It might sound funny to an outsider, but this stadium is sacred ground to our family. We grew up here. We've spent Thanksgiving and Christmas days here when there were games. And this space we're in now—this space is *family only*. We've stuck to those rules since we bought this box. No press. No outsiders. You being here means he's let you in, and my little brother doesn't let anyone in. I'm asking you for your help, which, if you knew me, you'd know isn't something I do often, or well . . . ever."

"You might not like me after this," I warn. "I'm pretty sure Jace feels smothered. I've only known all of you for a few hours, and you guys are a whole lot to take in, for someone like me who grew up with a really small family. But your brother smiles when he talks about his family. The smile drops, though, when he talks about feeling like he's being controlled. It sounds like he's got a reason to be mad."

"I want you to think about how you feel holding Cohen. Then think about watching him grow up and all the times you'll help him deal with the shit life throws at him. Then imagine suddenly, you're told you have to stop taking care of him. I was eleven when Jace was born and twenty-three when his mom died. Back then, Lenny and I were the only other women in the house, and Lenny left for Oxford the next year. I've been overprotective of him his entire life and I doubt that's going to change."

"What would you have done at twenty-three if someone tried to control your life for you? Not just tried to tell you what to do—but did it for you without asking."

Scarlet doesn't answer me, an impassive mask covering her face.

"I think you need to tell Jace all this. Not me."

"He won't talk to me," she finally says, and the mask begins to crumble, showing glimpses of a sister scared of losing her brother.

"Well, *that* I can help with." I stand with Cohen sound asleep in my arms and look around until my eyes lock with Jace's. It takes only a tiny tilt of my head for him to cross the room.

"Everything okay over here?" he asks as I push him into my vacated seat and hand him Cohen. I squeeze his shoulder and offer a reassuring smile, hoping he's not too mad about my ambush. "I want to get a bottle ready before we have to leave."

"Cohen's sleeping," Jace answers, completely confused.

"I know. But better to be safe than sorry." And as I walk away, I hope I didn't just cross the line.

~

*J*ace

"She's pretty incredible, Jace. I don't remember the last time somebody handled us that well. We're not exactly an easy bunch." Scarlet is quiet as she talks, not wanting to be overheard by the servers who've started taking down the buffet next to us.

"Yeah. I figured that out the first time I met her months ago when she wouldn't give me her name." I move my gaze from Indy on the other side of the room back to my oldest sister, trying to maintain my calm. "What do you want, Scarlet?"

"I want to apologize."

"Could you repeat that?" I don't think I've ever heard Scarlet apologize. To anyone.

"I'm sorry. You were right. You're a grown man, and I'm not your mom." Her voice cracks quietly on the last word.

"I love you, Scar. But you've got to give me some room to breathe."

She wipes at her eye, then reaches over and runs a hand over Cohen's back. "I'll give you room. But it won't be easy for me, Jace. I'm used to taking care of everything. I think control might be my love language."

"You want to babysit so I can take my nanny out on a date then? You can have complete control for the night." I lean over and kiss Scarlet's temple. "What are you going to do to me if I tell everyone you apologized?"

Scarlet cocks a perfectly arched black brow. "Do you really want to go there?"

"Nah . . . Just teasing you. In all seriousness, I reached out to your private investigator."

"And . . . ?"

"He just filled me in on everything you already know, which isn't much," I tell her, frustrated.

"We'll find her, Jace."

# INDIA

$\mathcal{A}$s the car comes to a stop in Jace's driveway, he runs a hand over my head, tugging on my hair. "Thanks for coming with me tonight."

"Of course," I mumble as I hurry out of the car to take Cohen upstairs. "Time for a bath and bed, little man."

Jace and I need to talk, but I have no idea how that'll go.

Maybe I'm using Cohen as a buffer, or maybe I'm a coward who's petrified that by speaking with his sister, I overstepped, ruining any chance at having an *us* before we ever really got a chance.

Once I have Cohen situated, we sink into the soft, chenille rocker in the corner of his room, snuggled up with a bottle. Big navy-blue eyes grow heavy with each pull of the formula. "Did you know I didn't want to be a nanny?" I whisper to the beautiful boy in my arms, finding it hard to believe it's barely been a week since my interview. "I almost didn't take this job."

I think about how close I came to blowing off my interview and how happy I am that I didn't. "It's pretty crazy the way one week can change your life."

And your heart.

"Yeah, it is." Jace stands in the open door, his arms stretched over his head, leaning against the door frame. Thick muscles flex in his biceps, testing the limits of his sleeves.

It's entirely unfair how attractive he is, and how easy he makes it look.

"My brother didn't want me to take this job," I whisper. "He was worried I'd give up on my dreams."

"Then here I am, the asshole who made you sign a twelve-month contract."

"You were being a good daddy. That's what you're supposed to do. Cohen comes first." Formula dribbles out of the corner of the sweet boy's mouth when I pull the bottle free. His tiny lips still pursed and sucking an imaginary nipple, completely content.

"Scarlet said something earlier that's been playing on a loop all night." I gather Cohen in my arms and stand, inhaling slowly and pressing my lips to his forehead. "About how hard it is to let go."

"Then don't let go." Jace takes Cohen from me, hugs him tightly to his chest, then lays him gently in his bed. When he turns back, the longing in his eyes is magnetic, pulling me to him like he's my true north. *Maybe he is.*

He grabs the monitor, then my hand and pulls me through his bedroom and out onto the balcony. Stars light up the inky night's sky, and fireflies dance in the darkness. Jace sits down on an oversized lounge chair, then tugs me down between his legs. My back presses against his hard chest as he wraps his arms around me. "Do you hear that? It's the falls crashing against Kroydon Lake."

His lips brush over my temple before moving to my ear. "That used to be my favorite sound until I heard Cohen laugh."

He snakes a hand under my shirt and skims his rough, warm palm against my cool skin. "Now, are you going to tell me what's bothering you?"

I close my eyes and rest my head against his shoulder. "I'm sorry if I overstepped with Scarlet. I tried to tell her to talk to you, but she wouldn't take no for an answer. I didn't like ambushing you."

"Pretty girl, you didn't overstep. Scarlet and I needed to talk, and now we have. It's over. We've moved on." He rests his chin on my shoulder and leans his head against mine, his warm minty breath fanning my face, sending goosebumps dancing down my spine.

"Really? Just like that?" I turn in his arms and sit on my knees to face him. But I should have known that wouldn't be enough for Jace. He pulls me forward until I'm straddling his legs, those two big palms splayed out on my thighs.

"Just like that. I don't like holding grudges unless you're my opponent on the ice. Then I'll make you my bitch."

"Oh really?" I counter. "Does that mean you're talking to Max now too? Because it looked like you were avoiding each other all night."

"Max is different," Jace groans. "He still thinks he did the right thing."

"By drafting you?"

"Yeah. He thinks he was justified. I think he's a stubborn asshole with a God complex."

"Max is the oldest, right? It's Max, then Scarlet?" I'm not sure why I'm pushing this, but it feels like the right thing to do.

"Yeah. Max is the oldest. Dad's protégé. He stepped into our father's shoes when Dad died. But he's never going to be Dad."

I rest my hands on Jace's broad shoulders, loving the way his muscles bunch under my touch. "Maybe he's not trying to be your dad. Maybe he's just doing whatever it takes to keep his family together. *Maybe* he's trying to not let go."

"Low blow, using my words against me. That's exactly what he's doing, but it's different. And I'm not okay with it. I don't like feeling like a puppet." Jace's hands slide up my ribs under my shirt, wrapping around me and pulling me closer. "You really want to talk about my brother?"

"I guess not," I tell him and kiss his cheek. "Would it be okay if I took Cohen into town? I'd like to pop into The Bee and introduce him to Gramps. Maybe stop into Sweet Temptations and see if Sophie's working. Walk over to the park, so we're not cooped up all day."

"Sure. Just do me a favor and take the SUV. The keys are in the kitchen." He drags a hand up to my neck and runs his thumb over my wildly beating pulse.

I squirm against the growing erection nestled between my thighs, trying to focus on our conversation and not on how good I know he can make me feel. "I have a car, Jace. I don't need yours."

His eyes sparkle as his smile grows devious. "Mine's bigger."

When I hold back a laugh, he flashes a devilish smirk. "And safer. Get your mind out of the gutter, naughty girl. I was talking about the car."

"Sure you were," I tease.

"You're going to be a handful, aren't you?" He pulls my shirt over my head and presses a kiss to my heart.

I yank his shirt a little less gracefully from his body. "I guess it's a good thing you've got big hands." I try not to overthink as I scrape my nails down along his chest and over his abs. Reaching inside his shorts, I wrap my hand around his thick cock and stroke it once. Then a second time before I shimmy off the chair and down to my knees, tugging his shorts down his legs and looking up through fluttering lashes. This man is all mine. "It's my turn to taste you, Jace."

He gathers my hair in my hands and wraps it around his fist. Gently tugging, he forces my eyes up to his. "Are you going to take me in your mouth like a good girl, baby?"

I nod, desperate for a taste, then flatten my tongue and slowly lick my way up his velvety-smooth cock, like he's the most decadent thing I've ever tasted . . . because he is. A groan vibrates from his chest, visceral and sexy, sending a bolt of longing straight to my already-drenched sex. "You keep telling me I'm yours, Jace," I gasp with so much need. "But I need to know you're mine too."

"You're fucking right, I'm yours. Now show me." He tugs my hair and groans as I wrap my hand around the base of his cock, unable to get my fingers all the way around it. I hollow my cheeks and swallow him down, inch by hard inch. My eyes water, and my throat closes at the invasion.

Running his hands through my hair, Jace pets and caresses and praises me, using the dirtiest words I've ever heard. Tears pool in my eyes. I mindlessly push my own hand into my panties and rub my index and middle fingers around my clit. Frantic for my own release.

"Good girl. Touch your clit and get yourself ready for me, Indy. But don't you dare come yet. I own your orgasms, baby."

Oh fucking hell. I gag as my concentration goes to shit since his words incinerated every brain cell I have and ratcheted my need even higher, then whimper in protest when Jace pulls out of my mouth.

"Do you want me to take care of you, baby?"

I nod, unable to form words. Jace pulls a condom from his pocket and sheathes himself. Before I realize it, he's pick me up, wrapped my legs around his waist, shoved my shorts to the side, and slammed inside me.

I'm limp in his arms, unable to move or think or do anything but chase the orgasm that's bright and sparking and ready to explode into a thousand flames around us both.

"Come for me, Indy. I want to feel that pussy pulse around me. I want you to feel me every time you move tomorrow. I want you to never forget who owns those orgasms . . . Give it to me."

And as if there was any way my body could deny his command, fireworks explode behind my eyes, and I cling to him, begging . . . pleading . . . shouting out his name.

# JACE

*I*ndy and I stayed locked in our own bubble for the rest of the weekend. It was easy to fall into the new routine during the day. But at night, we'd go outside under the stars and get lost in each other.

Discovering all the ways to make my pretty girl moan was intoxicating, but waking up with her wrapped around me each morning was different . . . It was peaceful.

And *peace* hasn't been something I've had much experience with.

Today was the first morning I had to leave her for work, and it sucked way worse than I expected. Indy and Cohen were curled up on the couch. My boy looked at her like she was his whole world. I understand that feeling.

I thought about sticking around the house, not ready for our bubble to burst. But it's Monday morning, and I told Connor I'd meet the guys today. Fifteen minutes later, I pull into a nearly empty parking lot, grab my gear from the backseat, and head into the locker room.

Low voices carry as I drop my gear on the bench.

Connor and Coach O'Doul round the corner and stop when they see me.

"Kingston," O'Doul barks in his gruff voice. The man is a living hockey legend. He's spent twenty years coaching the Revolution, and that was after retiring as a Hall of Fame right winger for a team that won five cups back-to-back. He's older and broader, but I have no doubt Coach could hang with us on the ice if he needed to. "Coming to skate with the team?"

"Coach." I shake his hand. "Just trying to get more time in before preseason starts."

"Good. The sooner we can start working the on-ice chemistry, the better. Get your legs under you, son, and get ready for your first season in the pros."

"Thanks, Coach. That's the plan."

Coach pats my arm and nods at Connor. "Don't go easy on the rookie."

The two of us watch Coach leave before Connor turns to me. "Ready to get your ass handed to you, rookie?"

"I guess I am."

~

We ran drills for the next two hours with a few guys from the team. Connor, Boone, and me against Douglas, Walker, and Gagné.

"That all you got, rookie?" Walker taunts when he slams me into the boards. He's the team enforcer. The fighter. And he's sure as shit the guy who has a problem with me.

"What's your problem, Walker?" I shove him away without calling attention to us.

"You're my problem, rookie. Pretty boy, rich kid whose brother bought him a team and a spot while the rest of us had to come up through the minors and earn ours." Walker's been on this team for-fucking-ever. Great to know he's bought into everything the press has put out there.

"You're wrong," I seethe.

"Then prove it."

We skate back to center ice, and I line up next to Boone.

"Damn, rookie. I'm gonna love not being the new guy this year," Boone laughs, like he's only just realized he no longer holds that miserable role. He's the left wing to my center with Connor on my right. The three of us have already fallen into an easy line, reminding me of everything I love about this game.

"Watch it, Boone. You've only got one season on Kingston. You're not exactly an old-timer yet." Connor drops the puck for Gagné and me to fight it out. Games can be won and lost with first touches, and Gagné and I have been battling it out all morning. Each of us winning as many as we've lost. And there's something about going toe-to-toe with one of your idols that's pretty fucking amazing.

When we're walking off the ice after the last drill, muscles burning and soaked in sweat, Gagné stops me. "You did well today, rookie." Even after spending his entire eleven-year career playing in Philadelphia, his French-Canadian accent is still thick. "You've got heart and speed and skill. And from what Cap said, you've got discipline in spades. Don't let the press force you to play their game. And ignore Walker. He doesn't like anyone."

"Thanks man. I'll try."

*~*

I follow Connor and Boone onto Main Street to grab lunch after practice, and when we pull into the parking lot behind The Busy Bee again, I shake my head and get out of my car. "Seriously, man. Do you come here every day?"

"Don't knock it till you try it, rookie." Boone slaps a hand down on my shoulder. "Great food, and no one bothers us here."

"Yeah, Cap brought me here last week." I look Connor's way and don't miss his smile at me calling him *Cap*. The fucker is the captain of the team, after all. And I can show respect when it's earned.

Connor walks through the door. "Fuck off. I eat here a lot. I don't like to cook."

We take the same booth we did last week. "Do you guys live in town or in the city?"

Connor passes menus to Boone and me. "I bought a house ten minutes from here on the other side of town last year."

"Yeah, and I've been renting from him since then." Boone closes his menu and flashes a big, goofy grin when Gladys comes to take our order.

"You're supposed to be looking for your own place, man," Connor sighs.

"You know you'd miss me, asshole. Who'd do your laundry if I left?"

"Wait." I look between them, shocked. "You do his laundry?"

"Nah." Boone leans back against the booth and looks around. "But I pay for the cleaning lady who does. Besides, he bought a giant house on the lake. He'd be lonely without me." He bats his eyelashes like a cartoon character, and Connor shoves him away.

"Dick. I bought the big house for privacy. Not so I could wake up to you drinking the orange juice out of the container."

"What can I say? I like OJ." Boone grabs the strawberry

milkshake Gladys places in front of him and passes us the chocolate ones. Guess I'm a regular now too.

"Wait. You guys live on Kroydon Lake? How have I never seen you? I've lived on Lakeside Drive for most of this year. My brothers own half the damn neighborhood."

"I live in Falls Terrace on the other side of the lake," Connor says before my eyes catch on the beautiful blonde holding my baby and walking through the swinging kitchen door.

I stand, the guys suddenly forgotten behind me at the table. "Hey, pretty girl."

Indy's big doe eyes sparkle before a beautiful smile spreads across her pretty face. "Hey, handsome. What are you doing here?"

An older man, who's built like a damn bull, growls through a long rectangular kitchen window behind the counter. "Why are you calling her *pretty girl?*"

"Gramps," she laughs. "This is Jace." She laces her fingers with mine and pulls me toward the counter. "Jace, this is my Grampa Carl."

Carl doesn't seem impressed. "So this is the young man who stole you away?"

Boone and Connor join us at the counter, not wanting to miss a chance to give me shit. "It's not nice to steal, Jace."

Teammate or not, I'm gonna kill Boone later.

"You two know this kid?" Carl growls.

"You know *them?*" I counter.

Indy hugs Boone and Connor, setting my nerves on edge. I don't like them touching her. "They've been regulars for ages."

Great. Boone moves into Indy's space, his hand moving to her back as he looks over Cohen. "And who's this tough guy?"

"Hands off my kid and my woman." I tug her to me.

"She's her own woman, you little pissant." Carl disappears from the window, then barges through the swinging door. "There's no ring on her finger. She's her own damn woman."

"My God. Could we all put our dicks away please? I think the health inspector would frown on a pissing contest in the middle of The Bee." Indy hands me Cohen, then tucks her arm through Carl's. "I *am* my own woman, Gramps." She looks up at me with hesitant eyes. "I'm also Jace's girlfriend."

Another groan from Carl. "Jesus Christ. It's been one week."

"As amusing as this is, people are staring," Gladys tells us all as she comes out of the kitchen with a tray of our food and herds us away. "Why don't you all go sit back down. And you,"—she glares at Carl—"there are orders piling up back there. Your granddaughter is the smartest young woman I know. Stop acting like a caveman and start trusting the girl you raised, old man."

"I'm three years younger than you, Gladys."

"But you look much older." She winks. "Now shoo."

I usher Indy back to our booth, where the four of us sit as Carl heads back into the kitchen. Gladys lays out our plates, obviously enjoying everyone's discomfort. "I'll be right back with the ketchup."

"I can grab it, Gladys," Indy offers.

"You don't work here anymore, young lady. Sit right there and eat your young man's fries, like I know you want to." Before any of us can say a thing, she's back with a bottle of ketchup and a twinkle in her eye. "Holler if you need anything else."

No one says anything for a minute until Cohen spits out his binky and squeals. Indy has it clipped to his shirt so it doesn't fall to the floor, and I pop it back in without looking at either of my teammates. "Is he hungry?"

"No. He shouldn't be. I think he just wants attention," she answers quietly.

When I finally look at Connor and Boone, they're both staring at us with their mouths hanging open. Boone's got a fry held midair. "What the fuck, Kingston? You got a baby?"

"Close your mouth, Boone, or I'll make sure Gramps puts you on the *Do Not Serve* list."

Connor grins. "Dude, Carl refused to serve Gagné for a full fucking month last year after he questioned his poutine. Better shut your mouth."

"Fuck off, Cap." Boone points his fry at Indy. "When the hell were you pregnant?"

"I wasn't." She rolls her eyes. "You've come in every week for the past year. Don't you think that's something you'd have noticed?"

"So, you and Kingston are . . ." Connor leaves the sentence open-ended, waiting for Indy to fill in the blank, and it seems like the most important question anyone's asked.

Leave it to my girl to keep us all on our toes.

She steals one of my fries, dipping it in ketchup before popping it in her mouth. Her lips tip up on one side before she answers, "We're none of your business unless Jace wants to make it your business."

"She's mine," rolls off my tongue before Boone or Connor get any crazy ideas. "She and Cohen both are. He's the family stuff I was telling you about last week, Cap."

Connor whistles low and long. "Yeah. I guess you do have more on your plate than we realized. Congrats, man. He's beautiful." The fucker smirks. "They both are."

"Eyes to yourself, Connor. You don't want Gramps to add you to that list too, do you?"

"My loss, Indy."

"You bet your ass it is," I tell him, then push my plate to Indy.

She cuts the burger in half and hands me one side like it's any other day. "So how was practice?"

~

*A*fter lunch, I make arrangements with Boone and Connor for them to pick me up for practice tomorrow, and we say goodbye before Indy takes me back to the kitchen, which is now closed. The Bee is only open until three p.m. daily, and Carl is already sitting in his office, doing something on the computer, while a young kid cleans up in the kitchen.

"Gramps . . ." Indy knocks on the open door until Carl looks up and takes his glasses off.

"Come in, sweetheart." His entire demeanor changes when he sees Cohen and me next to her. "You can stay out in the hall."

"Gramps . . . Be nice." She pushes me through the door, then follows me in. "Jace, I'd like you to officially meet my grandfather."

"We've met," Carl grumbles, staring balefully at my outstretched hand.

"Gramps."

"Am I supposed to say *nice to meet you* to the boy who stole you away?"

Indy sighs and sits down in one of the two chairs across from Carl. She crosses her legs and primly rests her hands on his desk. When she stares at me, I'm pretty sure she's silently telling me to sit, so I follow her command.

Kinda like a dog who knows when his master is pissed-off but unsure if it's me she's pissed at.

"First, Jace is a grown man—not a boy. He owns his own home, has a college degree, and a good job. Stop insulting him just because you can. That's beneath you."

Carl opens his mouth to speak but stops as soon as she glares.

Damn. Scarlet could take pointers from my girl.

"And second, you know Jace didn't steal me away from anything. He offered me a job that he's paying me more than a fair wage to do. And before you say a single thing, no, I'm not being paid to be his girlfriend. That part is new. It's also not up for discussion. You always say you want me to be happy. Well, I'm happy. Period. Now be nice and shake his hand."

Carl grinds his teeth but does as this little spitfire says and shakes my hand.

"It's nice to meet you, sir," I offer.

"That's yet to be determined."

"Gramps . . ."

"Fine. You want me to be nice? I want you both at my house for dinner next week when Atlas comes home." He looks at Cohen, and I finally see a trace of a smile. "All three of you. Dinner, Friday night."

"Can we do it at Jace's instead? Please? It'll be easier with Cohen." Her voice is softer and sweeter, now that she wants something, and I think I might be watching a master class in manipulation. Damn. It's impressive. I feel like I should be taking notes.

I might be screwed for life, but I'm pretty sure I'll give her everything she wants anyway, no manipulation needed.

Carl's dark-brown eyes nail me to my seat. "You got plates that aren't paper and silverware that isn't plastic?"

"Yes, sir." Damn. I probably need to thank my sisters for stocking my house, after all.

"Fine. But I'm cooking at your house. I'll bring what we need."

"Thank you, Gramps." Indy leans over and squeezes his hand, but sweet old Grampa Carl holds his stare on me.

"Her brother is going to try to intimidate you. But I want you to remember something, son. I'm a retired marine. Anything Atlas threatens to do, I *can* do and get away with. I might be old, but I still know people."

Holy shit. This guy just threatened to kill me, and I'm not allowed to laugh.

"How about I promise if I ever do anything to hurt her, I'll take whatever punishment you give?"

"That's the first smart thing you've said all day."

~

SCARLET

My late meeting Wednesday just got canceled. I can be at your house by seven. Take the nanny out on a date Jace Joseph. I like her.

JACE

Seriously?

SCARLET

Do you want me to say no?

JACE

Nope. Thanks Scar.

# INDIA

*J*ace takes Cohen from me later that night and presses his lips to my forehead—something that seems to come so naturally to him—and my body relaxes at the tender contact. "I'm going to put Cohen to bed, then I'll be back down."

The little man's nighttime routine can take up to an hour, so I make myself a cup of Earl Grey tea, grab my Kindle and a blanket, then head outside. A cool breeze blows off the lake as I settle in an Adirondack chair and open Natalie Sinclair's newest romance. I usually love reading about her sexy football players, but after reading the same paragraph five times without retaining any of it, I give up and close the Kindle.

Listening to Jace claim me in front of his teammates earlier today . . . Hearing him declare I'm his over and over again. First to his brother, then his entire family, and now his team . . . It's equally overwhelming and incredibly intoxicating.

Fairy lights turn on, illuminating the trees surrounding the patio, and a slow, sultry beat plays from hidden speakers. A barefoot Jace approaches me, with old, worn jeans hanging from his hips and a faded black Philadelphia Kings t-shirt pulling tight across his chest. When he reaches me, he holds out his hand. "Dance with me, pretty girl."

"Well." I place my small hand in his large one and let him pull me to my feet. "When you ask so nicely."

Jace wraps a thick arm around my waist and covers his heart with our joined hands, strong and sure, warming my blood and my heart. "I'm not very good at asking, Indy." His deep voice is strained and gruff. "I've always been more of a *take what I want* kind of guy. But for you, I'll ask . . . *if* that's what you want."

"Funny enough . . . I kinda like it when you don't ask." My vision shifts and sharpens in that moment, and suddenly, I see Jace in a way I haven't before. I see the strong man standing in front of me, whose entire life changed two months ago. I see the man who's constantly carrying the weight of the world on his shoulders and yet wants to carry the weight of me and my issues too. I lay my head on his chest and whisper, "I trust you, Jace."

He kisses the crown of my hair, then rests his chin on my head. "I spoke with my sister Scarlet earlier. She can watch Cohen tomorrow night. Let me take you out on a real date. Just you and me for a few hours. It may be our only chance before the season starts."

~

*I* force my eyes open the next morning as the strains of a Foo Fighters song is sung over the baby monitor and sink further under a warm blanket, surrounded by Jace's crisp clean scent. I lie there for a minute, enjoying the sound of him singing to his son, and smile in contentment.

Eventually, I force myself up, throw on one of Jace's tees, and pad across the hall.

The early morning sun trickles in through the curtains, soaking Jace and Cohen in a stunning golden light, and the sight takes my breath away. I stop at the open door, unable to take my eyes off them, the pull too strong.

Jace glides in the chenille rocker, eyes closed and his feet propped up on the ottoman. Cohen sleeps softly and soundly on his bare chest.

"You've been hiding quite a voice, Kingston," I whisper softly as I step into the room. "If hockey doesn't work out for you, you could give Dave Grohl a run for his money."

A smile tugs at his full lips. "Are you going to yell at me for letting my little buddy here sleep on me instead of his bed, Nanny Indy?"

"No, handsome." I lift Cohen from Jace and carefully lay him down in his bed. When I turn back around, I offer him my hand like he did for me earlier and tug him to his feet. "Do you want some breakfast before practice?"

"Are you on the menu?" He wraps his arms around my waist and pulls my back against his chest, burying his face in my neck. "Because I could eat you all day."

I angle my head, giving him better access. "As tempting as that sounds, you've got practice today, and Cohen and I have plans."

"What are you two up to?" He wraps my hair around his fist and tips my head back, giving me all sorts of naughty ideas.

"We're going to see my friend Harper and maybe stop by Sweet Temptations. Now it's my turn to ask you a question . . ." I turn my head and smile. "What am I supposed to wear tonight?"

"Socks," he says with a wink.

I scrunch my nose and laugh. "Socks, huh?"

He steps back and smacks my ass. "Yup. Wear a good pair of socks. I'll see you tonight, pretty girl."

Socks . . .

INDY

Hey. Can you fit me in today? I need a new outfit. Something cute.

HARPER

Just come to my condo this afternoon. I have a closet full of things that'll fit you. My client should be done by 3 p.m.

INDY

Perfect! Thanks, Harps.

HARPER

And what exactly are we dressing you for, babe? I'll pull some things for you.

INDY

Jace asked me out on a date.

HARPER

Way to bury the lede. Hmm . . . maybe I should pull a few pieces from Le Desir too.

INDY

Maybe you should.

HARPER

India Marie Monroe. Are you going to let Jace Kingston see your no-no parts?

INDY

Who says he hasn't seen them already?

HARPER

Playing coy, Miss Monroe?

INDY

You're a lifesaver, Harps.

HARPER

See you soon.

❧

"Socks? That's all he said?" Harper asks as I follow her into her spare room she converted into an enormous walk-in closet a few months ago.

"Yup. That's it. Just that I should wear *socks*." I run my hand along her white shelves lined with shoes and handbags and eye a beautiful pair of red-soled heels. "Maybe he has a Catholic schoolgirl kink."

"Oh, Indy." Harper's eyes light up with excitement. "We could absolutely do something with that."

"I was kidding, Harps," I roll my eyes and shift Cohen in my arms.

She lays a white, long-sleeved bohemian blouse on the center island. "You may have been, but I wasn't. I could get behind a little kink." Harper pulls out two different pairs of jeans, then adds a pair of dark-brown, knee-high riding boots to my growing pile. "I want you to try those on. Let's see which ones make your ass look better." She reaches over and adds a pair of knitted, white knee-high socks on top. "Can't forget these. Now give me the little guy and scoot."

"Thanks, Harps." I give a happy Cohen over to Harper and watch her melt for my little man.

When I pick up the pile, she hands me a hanger full of silk. "These too. Then come back out and let me see."

I blush furiously as I look at the expensive silk. Real silk, not the Target brand stuff I usually wear. "When did you get so bossy?"

141

"Listen, small humans might be your expertise, but clothing is mine." She follows me into her room and sits on the bed, lying Cohen down next to her and tickling his tummy until his contagious laughter has us both smiling like loons.

Harper points at me. "You're going to look classy, sexy, and confident in your own skin because you, India Monroe, are all those things. My job is to just emphasize that. Now, go get changed."

I close her bathroom door behind me and strip out of my clothes, then slide on the white silk and lace cheeky panties and matching bra. When I look at myself in the mirror, adjusting the fit and smoothing my hands over my curves, I'm impressed. She's good.

"Let me know how the lingerie fits," she calls out. "The ladies at Le Désir just added me to their influencer team, so now, I get early access to all their new lines."

"They fit great, Harps," I offer weakly. When she pops her head in the doorway, I blush. "Harps . . ."

"You're smoking hot, Indy. Now stop being a nervous wreck and put the clothes on. What time is he taking you out tonight?" She plugs in her curling wand and pulls out her makeup bag, bouncing Cohen as she moves. "We've got a date to get you ready for."

"I'm not sure how to thank you, Harper."

"That's easy. With a big cup of coffee and all the dirty details tomorrow morning," she laughs.

The coffee I've got covered.

The details I think I'll hold onto, just for myself, a little longer.

# JACE

*I* hit Indy's number on speed dial, then wait.

"Hey, Jace." I hear the smile in her voice when she answers.

"Hey, pretty girl. Scarlet got here early. You almost home?" I ask and turn away from my sister and her prying eyes.

"The little man and I are on our way back now. We should be there in five minutes."

"Sounds good. See you in a few." I end the call, shove the phone in my pocket, and turn back around to, no doubt, face the firing squad.

"You really have it bad, don't you?" Scarlet leans on the kitchen counter with a cup of coffee in hand. "You're doing that thing"—she points at me—"with your face. My broody baby brother is smiling. That's something I haven't seen a lot of lately."

"Yeah. I guess I do." I grab her cup and take a sip of her coffee. "Seriously, how long did it take for you to know Cade was the one?"

Now it's Scarlet's turn to smile like the woman in love

she's been for years. My sister is the biggest ball-buster there is until you get her talking about her husband or her kids. "I think I knew when I was in high school, but I didn't fight for us back then. Thankfully, we got our second chance." She kicks my foot with her pointy-toed stiletto. "You know . . . your mom used to give great advice about falling in love."

"I remember."

She kicks me again. "Follow your instincts, little brother. I'm not going to tell you what to do. Cade and I screwed it up plenty before we got it right. But I'm glad we didn't give up. So take from that what you want." She shrugs out of her suit coat, kicks off her heels, and throws her long, dark hair up on top of her head. "Now then, I'm going to go change so I can snuggle up with my nephew as soon as he gets home."

"Thanks, Scar."

"Don't mention it . . . to anyone." She kisses my cheek, then walks into the other room as the door from the garage to the kitchen opens. In walks my girl, who looks like an absolute knockout, holding my kid.

My whole fucking world, right there in front of me.

I take Cohen's car seat from her with one hand and cup her cheek with the other.

"Hi," she murmurs before pressing up on her toes and brushing her lips over mine.

Electricity arcs between us as I slip my hand into her hair. "You look fantastic," I tell her before deepening the kiss, needing another taste. When she sighs sweetly against my mouth, I slide my tongue along hers, ready to drown in this woman who feels so fucking right in my hands.

I put Cohen down and have her up against the counter and panting, my hands on her ass, when a throat clears behind us.

"You two better get out of here before I pop some popcorn and watch." Scarlet unbuckles Cohen from his seat and holds him up for me. "Now, kiss your son and get out of here."

"Thanks, Scar." I kiss Cohen and take Indy's hand. "Ready, pretty girl?"

"Am I allowed to know where we're going yet?" She squeezes my hand as I escort her to the SUV. Her addictive scent catches on the breeze as her hair blows in my face. It's vanilla and something else. Warm and spicy sweet. My mouth waters for another taste.

I open her door and eye her. A white ruffle peeks out over the tops of her brown boots as she sits down. "I like the socks."

Her eyes crinkle with her smile as she pulls those shapely legs into the car. "You don't have some kind of schoolgirl kink, do you, Kingston?"

"What?" I laugh as I lean in and kiss her until she's gasping for breath. "Jesus, baby. You in a uniform? I mean, I wouldn't say no. But you're the fantasy. Not what you're wearing."

"I'll have to remember that for later." She rubs her thumb over my bottom lip. "Now, are you going to tell me where we're going?"

I shut the door and round the car, then get in, running my hands over her hair. "We're going to my favorite place."

"You're not playing fair, Kingston."

"Just trust me, pretty girl." We pull out of our neighborhood and drive the short distance to the Revolution's practice facility. The same ice I've been skating on since I laced up my first skates.

When we pull into the parking lot, she turns toward me, laughing. "Are you bringing me to work, Jace Kingston?"

I swear to God, just the way she says my name . . . I'm so gone for this woman.

"I'm bringing you to my sanctuary, baby."

Moments later, the two of us walk hand in hand into the rink, where old man McGovern is waiting for us. He hands me the keys. "Everything's set up for you, kid. Make sure you lock up when you're done."

"Thanks, Mr. McGovern."

Indy's face lights up as the doors swing shut behind him. "You *did* bring me to work."

"Let's get some skates on you, pretty girl. I wanna see you fly." We walk into the locker room, and I grab her hips, lifting her onto the bench, then run my hands down her delectable legs. I finger her ruffled socks, then drag down the zippers on her boots and toss them aside. "Good girl. I like the socks."

Her fingers turn white as her breath hitches and her legs tremble. "So, tell me . . . Why here? What makes this your favorite place in the world?"

I grab the white ice skates from the counter and slide the first one on her foot. "My mom used to bring us here when we were little and needed to burn off energy. She'd always ask who wanted to come. Lenny hated falling down. Ice skating was never her thing. Hudson was into martial arts. Sawyer was always at swim practice. Scarlet despised anything that made her sweat. So it was always Becks, Max, and me."

I lace up her first skate before doing the same to the other. "They were so much bigger than me. Always faster. Until eventually, they weren't. But that took years." I kiss her palm, then put on my own skates before standing her up. "But I loved being here with them. It was fun and exciting, and it gave me a reason to be with my cool big brothers."

I kiss her quickly and squat down to check her laces. "How do they feel?"

"Good, I guess." She takes a tentative, wobbly step, then another.

"Ready to try out the ice?"

She grabs my hand. "Maybe . . ."

"I've got you, baby." When the words slip past my lips so easily, I realize how much I mean them. "I won't let you fall."

We step onto the ice, and I push off, pulling a shrieking Indy with me.

"That's it. Just hold on to me."

"Oh God. Okay . . ." She tries to match my stride but ends up scrambling instead. "Ahh . . . don't let go."

"I won't. Just hold on to me." We make our way slowly around the ice, her pale skin pink from the chill, and her smile growing with every small push off her blades. "That's it. You're getting it."

"When did you go from liking skating to loving it?" she asks as we round a corner, and my girl holds on for dear life.

"Mom signed me up for my first team when I was seven, and I never looked back. Until this year, it's always been where I felt the most at peace. The most free." I pull her to a stop and back her up against the boards as she laughs. "Until this summer. Until Cohen. Until you."

"Jace . . ." Her hand flies up to my face, a shaky thumb tracing my lips. "Remember when I said I didn't want this job?"

I kiss the pad of her thumb, swirling my tongue around it, then lifting her to sit on the edge of the boards. "I remember."

"I'm so glad I did it, Jace. I'm so glad you and Cohen came into my life. So much so, it scares me." I run my hand up her back between her shoulder blades and pull her toward me. "This all scares me. How much I feel . . . and how quickly I felt it. How sure of it I am. How is this possible?"

"You're not alone, baby. We're in this together. You know that. I've been telling you that since day one. I'm falling in love with you, India Monroe." I lift her from the boards and

147

skate around the rink again with her clinging to me like a koala bear.

When I speed up, she screams, "Oh my God, Jace. Put me down."

"As you wish." I drop my hold on her thighs for just a second, and her shrieks threaten to burst my eardrums.

"No, wait. Don't." Her nails dig into my back. "Don't drop me."

"Never, baby." We take another corner before I spin us around and skate backward. "Hold tight."

When Indy grips me tighter, I brush my lips over her ear. "Good girl."

Indy's watch beeps, and she silences it, then sighs. "I need to get something out of my purse."

I skate us over to the exit and off the ice, carrying her back into the locker room. "Want to tell me what that alarm is?"

She sits down on the bench and opens her purse, then pulls out a pill bottle and pops one into her mouth, never taking her eyes off me. "I have to take this every day. It's my evening pill, and I have to take it twelve hours after my morning one. I'm supposed to take it with food. The easiest way to do that is with the alarm." She pulls out a granola bar. "And I always have one of these in my bag."

"Smart and beautiful." I kiss her lips. "Are you ready for dinner then?"

"Starving. What are you feeding me?"

So many filthy thoughts are on the tip of my tongue. But instead, I take off my skates and slide my shoes back on, then help Indy with hers and pull her to her feet. She reaches up and smooths her thumb over my bottom lip. "Thank you for bringing me here. For sharing this with me."

She presses up on her toes and sucks my bottom lip between hers. "I'm falling in love with you, Jace."

My heart soars at her words, and I press her against the lockers. "Indy . . ." I groan, molding my hands to her ass and swallowing her moan.

"Have you ever had sex in a locker room, Kingston?" She licks into my mouth and wraps her hands around my neck.

"No, pretty girl. This is a sacred space."

She pulls away and tries to drop her legs, but I tighten my grip on her and growl, "If you think that means I don't want you, right here and now, you're fucking wrong. The space is sacred, but it doesn't hold a candle to you."

In the next breath, we're a tangle of hands and lips.

My pants are shoved down, then hers.

Her warm hands wrap around my cock, and she runs it through her drenched sex.

I hiss in a breath. "Shit, Indy. I don't have a condom."

Pressing her lips to my neck, she rocks my world. "I'm on the shot, but I understand if you don't want to—"

I cut her off by pushing my cock into her tight body. Wet and warm and gripping me like a fucking vice. "Holy fuck, baby, you feel incredible." My vision darkens. "I've never been bare before. I'm clean."

She covers my mouth with her hand and drops her head back against the locker as I move inside her. "I don't want to hear about anyone else. You're not the only one in this relationship who's possessive, handsome."

"Oh, baby." I spin us around and sit on the bench with her straddling my legs. "If you can think that hard, I'm doing something wrong." I thrust up inside her and press my thumb down on her clit until she's moaning in my arms and rocking her hips.

Her hands sink into my hair as she presses her tits to my chest, trying to get closer, taking what she wants.

What she needs.

Her soft hair falls forward, framing us like silk, and it's just the two of us, lost in the moment. "Indy."

Our eyes meet, and our connection sizzles as lightning pulls at the base of my spine.

"Oh God, Jase. I'm gonna come." She throws her head back as the walls of her pussy clench around me, pulling me deeper.

"That's it, baby." I fuck up into her, pistoning my hips until I feel her shatter around me, then fill her with my come. "Fuck . . ."

Indy lies there, sated in my arms, her head tucked against my chest as we both try to catch our breath. "Jace . . ."

"Yeah, pretty girl?"

"You've fucked me. Now, feed me," she giggles.

~

Thirty minutes later, my girl finishes half of a Fat Cat sandwich from the food trucks around the corner from the rink, and I stare in awe. It's a double cheeseburger—lettuce, tomato, mayo, ketchup, and french fries all on a bun. I'm impressed.

"I've gotta tell you, Jace." She wipes her lips with a paper napkin. "This is the best thing I've ever had in my mouth."

I groan and shake my head. "Do you do that on purpose?" I scrunch my sandwich wrapper into a ball and throw it in the trash. "Seriously. You set me up to say the filthiest things. It's getting harder to bite my tongue, baby."

She holds the remainder of her sandwich up to me, biting her lip. "Do you want a taste?"

I lean down and nip her ear instead. "I'd rather take a bite of you."

"What's stopping you then? Certainly not me." She

surprises me by shooting the rest of her sandwich into the trash without even looking.

"Aren't you just full of surprises?" I taunt.

She fists the front of my shirt. "You get good at trash-can basketball when you're stuck in a hospital for weeks. There isn't a lot to do, so you find ways to occupy yourself."

I groan long and deep. "Come on . . ."

"Go ahead and say it, Jace," she laughs and swings our hands as we walk back to the car.

"I can think of a few ways to keep you occupied, baby. Long and deep and hard happen to be my specialty." I laugh. "Look . . . I'm trying to be good."

"Maybe I like when you're bad," she teases.

"How do you feel about ice cream?" I ask as we get into the car.

"What do you have in mind, Kingston?" Her golden eyes glow with excitement.

So much, pretty girl.

So much.

# INDIA

*J*ace's thumb draws lazy circles on my thigh during the short drive home. His touch sends electricity pulsing through my already over-heated blood. It's the kind of touch that holds a promise. And I can't wait to pick up where we left off last night.

But when we walk inside the house, Scarlet is pacing the family room, attempting to calm a screaming Cohen. Thoughts of anything else disappear as a knot forms in my stomach.

Jace flies across the room, scooping Cohen out of her arms and cradling him to his chest. "What happened?"

"He woke up about an hour ago with a fever. I gave him some Infants' Tylenol, but he's been crying since then." She presses her hand to Cohen's head. "I doubt it's anything worth worrying about, but I'd call the pediatrician in the morning."

Jace pulls his phone from his pocket, then holds it up to his ear. "Hey, Wren. Cohen's got a fever. Can you come over and check him out?" He looks over at Scarlet and me, then back down at Cohen. "Thanks. See you in a minute."

"He's a baby, Jace. Babies get fevers. They don't require a house call." A clearly amused Scarlet kisses Cohen, then Jace before turning to me. "Take care of them. I'm not sure who's in for a worse night, Cohen or his daddy. Try not to let my brother lose his shit over a 100.1 degree fever." She hugs me, then pulls back. "Call if you need me."

~

*T*wo hours and one house call later, Cohen has an ear infection and a prescription Jace has run to the all-night pharmacy to get filled. I'm curled up on the couch with Cohen asleep on my chest when Jace walks back through the door. I lift my finger to my lips, silently telling Jace to be quiet.

I just got the little man calm enough to sleep. His breathing is still ragged from his cries, and his little chest rises and falls against mine.

Jace drops the prescription on the coffee table, then sits down next to me, draping his arm along the back of the couch. His fingers massage the base of my skull as he leans over and kisses my cheek. "How long has he been out?"

"Maybe five minutes," I tell him quietly.

Jace just sits and watches us for a long few minutes.

Cohen's drool drips down my chest, and Jace's eyes track its path. "I've never seen you in a tank top, pretty girl."

"Yeah well, I figured the skin on skin would feel good for Cohen, and the scar is already outta the bag, so no use trying to hide it anymore."

The glare Jace throws my way leaves no doubt he didn't like my little tease. "You never needed to hide it in the first place. Not from me."

And the thing is, for the first time in years, I don't feel like I have to hide .

Not from Jace.

Maybe not from anyone.

I lean my head against his arm and close my eyes. "I think it's going to be a long night."

"Not exactly for the reasons I'd hoped," he chuckles softly.

"We've got all the time in the world for that." I kiss the top of Cohen's sweet head and enjoy the feel of Jace's arms wrapping around me.

"Yeah, baby. We do."

～

*A*t some point during the night, Jace put Cohen down in his own bed, and he and I climbed onto the daybed on the other side of Cohen's room. We both crashed as soon as our heads hit the pillows. And the next morning, after a second dose of his antibiotic and more Tylenol, the little man seems to be feeling a little better.

By nine-thirty, once he's had a bottle, a bath, some tummy time, and is happily swaying in his swing while I nurse a cup of tea, there's a knock at the door.

"Honey . . . I'm home," Becket calls out as he walks into the kitchen with Boone and Connor behind him. "And I brought the kids."

"Umm . . . good morning," I offer, already exhausted.

"Hey, Indy." Boone winks as he eyes the coffee pot sitting on the counter. "Can I get a cup of that? Someone's decided it's not healthy, and he doesn't want to buy it anymore."

"Sure." I grab him a mug and push the sugar across the counter.

Connor groans. "Dude. You're a grown man. Buy it yourself."

"You guys fight like an old married couple. You realize

that, right?" I ask as Jace walks into the room and presses his lips to my temple.

"Morning, beautiful," he whispers so our audience doesn't hear him.

Cohen squeals from his swing as I pull back from his daddy.

Becks clears his throat, then smacks his brother's chest with a legal-sized manilla envelope. "Here are the documents you asked for."

"Thanks, man. I appreciate it."

"I'm adding it to your bill." He turns toward me. "Pleasure as always, Indy." Then he pulls me in with a menacing grin on his handsome face. "Wanna see Jace's head explode?"

"Get your hands off her, asshole," Jace shoves Becks away, and Boone and Connor laugh.

Hysterically.

Becks kisses my cheek. "Told ya."

This time it's my turn to shove him away, giggling.

Jace growls again, and Becks backs up, hands raised in surrender. "If you ever get bored with jack-off here, I'm just a call away." He takes a step back. "Just sayin'."

"Go, Becks. Before you can't say anything else," Jace threatens, and I roll my lips, trying not to smile. I guess Becks is an instigator.

We follow him into the other room and watch him stop when he opens the front door. "You've got a stray at the door," he tells us before stepping aside.

A distinctly southern lilt floats past him. "Oh, bless your heart." Harper steps around Becks, and I don't miss the way he watches her moving into the room before slamming the door shut behind him.

She walks right up to Jace and looks him over like she's examining a Triple-Crown-winning racehorse. Apparently pleased with what she sees, she holds out her hand. "You must be the infamous Jace Kingston."

"I am." Jace takes her hand. "And who exactly are you?"

She pastes on her best pageant queen smile while frick and frack behind us chuckle.

"Jace, this is one of my best friends, Harper Ellis. Harper, this is Jace." Then I twist and point to the guys. "And I think you've met Boone and Connor before."

She wiggles her fingers. "Hi'ya, boys."

It's not even ten a.m., and Harper is decked out in a strapless sundress that's belted and accentuating her tiny waist. Her strawberry-blonde hair is curled to perfection around her shoulders, and my feet hurt, looking at the heels she's wearing. Her grin grows when Jace looks at her like he doesn't know what to make of her. Not many people do the first time they meet Harper. "So nice to finally meet you, Jace."

"Yeah. You too," he tells her, not giving her a second look before kissing me. "You sure you're going to be okay with Cohen today?"

"We'll be fine." I try to convince this overprotective man. "I've got the numbers for Wren and the pediatrician if we need anything. Don't worry about us."

"Thank you," he whispers and presses his forehead to mine. "Take care of our boy and call me if you need anything." He shoulders his hockey bag. "We better get moving."

"Bye, boys," Harper calls out as the three of them leave. "Damn, Indy. That's a whole lot of man that just walked through that door. And if I'm not mistaken, I'd say he's a man in love."

"You're crazy, Harper. We've known each other for two weeks." But I didn't miss him calling Cohen *our boy*.

"Indy, I'm southern. We don't hide our crazy. We embrace

it." She wraps her arm around my shoulder and squeezes. "But crazy or not, I saw what I saw. That boy is in love."

I know we've said things in the heat of the moment, but still—falling in love doesn't necessarily mean actually *in love*.

It's not possible.

Not yet.

Is it?

# JACE

"*K*ingston, man. You're one lucky son of a bitch," Boone tells me as we climb into the SUV. "You got the girl. You got the kid. You got the job and the house. Although, I'd have at least enjoyed my rookie year before locking all that shit down. But you do you, boo."

"Pretty sure babies don't give a shit about your plans, shithead," Connor fires back.

"And how would you know, Cap?"

"You've met my nieces and nephews, moron," Connor groans while I ignore them both and scroll through the text chain Becks set off this morning.

BECKS

If Jace knocks Indy up, can Cohen and baby Kingston be Irish twins even if we're not Irish?

HUDSON

Damn, man. You move fast, kid.

LENNY

Not everyone takes two years to make their move, Huddy.

HUDSON

Not everyone lies the first time they meet their future spouse either, Lenny.

AMELIA

Hey! Why am I feeling attacked right now?

SCARLET

Must be something about those Beneventi boys.

LENNY

Don't be jealous, Scarlet. Green is not your color.

SCARLET

Don't be a bitch, Len. I pull it off way better.

MAX

We are Irish, asshole.

BECKS

I would know if we were Irish, Maxipad.

SCARLET

Your mother is half Irish, Becket.

BECKS

No she's not.

MAX

Yes she is, dumbass.

JACE

Fuck off, Becket.

AMELIA

Pretty sure Jace isn't the one with baby news . . .

LENNY

OMG! Are you and Sam having another baby?

JACE

Not it.

SCARLET

Nope. That ship has sailed its final voyage in my house.

HUDSON

Maddie still hasn't gotten over pushing Teagan out in our kitchen. It's definitely not us.

MAX

I picked up tampons for Daphne yesterday.

BECKS

There's so much wrong with that sentence, Max.

MAX

Fuck off, Becket. Real men buy their wives tampons.

HUDSON

Thought you'd get her maxipads, Maxipad.

BECKS

Ohh . . . Burn.

SCARLET

OMG

AMELIA

Hmmm . . . Guessing I'll keep my mouth shut then.

LENNY

Becks and Sawyer are the only ones not chiming in.

BECKS

Consider me chimed. Kendall is not pregnant.

LENNY

Thank fuck. When are you going to break up with Medusa?

SCARLET

Forget Medusa. Oh SAWYER . . .

JACE

Holy shit. Sawyer . . .

HUDSON

Damn . . . Sawyer

MAX

Just jumping in because apparently, I'm a follower. Sawyer – got something to tell the class?

SAWYER

WTF? We were going to tell you all at family dinner Sunday night.

JACE

We're doing family dinner Sunday?

SCARLET

Focus, Jace.

AMELIA

Blame your wife. She smelled the coffee at Sweet Temptations this morning and turned green. When I asked her if she needed a decaf, she told me to fuck off, then said yes please. That's a pregnant woman if I've ever seen one.

SAWYER

You used to be the nice one.

**AMELIA**

It was an act.

**SCARLET**

The Kings are playing at one on Sunday.
Looks like family dinner is at the stadium.

"*D*ude, you waiting for an invitation or do you think maybe you want to get the hell out of the car?"

I look up from the phone to see Boone staring at me.

"Fuck. Sorry. I'm coming." I shove my phone in my pocket and follow them into the rink.

"Get your shit together, rookie, before you get your ass handed to you. I don't want to have to tell your pretty girlfriend I broke you." Cap smirks.

"Stop looking at my pretty girlfriend, Cap, and I might not embarrass you in front of your team."

"You can try."

I laugh and drop my bag down in the locker room. "Loser buys lunch?"

"Deal."

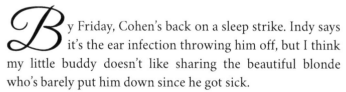

*B*y Friday, Cohen's back on a sleep strike. Indy says it's the ear infection throwing him off, but I think my little buddy doesn't like sharing the beautiful blonde who's barely put him down since he got sick.

He's become quite the cute little cockblocker, and I'm starting to think he likes her better than me. Not that I blame him. I'd spend all my time with my head on my girl's chest too if I could, but I can't because he's grown quite accustomed to it. Like I said. Cock. Block.

He's currently strapped to her chest in some kind of ribbon sling thing that's wrapped around her while she wipes down the kitchen counters.

I sneak up behind them and drop a kiss on Indy's shoulder. "Good morning, beautiful."

"Oh my God, Jace. You scared the shit out of me," she gasps, and I try to hide my laugh.

"Sorry, baby. I wanted to say goodbye before I left for practice. I'm not sure when I'll be back. What time is your family coming?"

"I think six-ish."

I run my hand over Cohen's head and watch his dark blue eyes stare up at me, so damn happy. "You take care of our girl, okay, bud?"

Goddamn, I like the sound of that.

She squeezes my arm, then shoves me away. "Go. You don't want to be late for your first official preseason practice."

I kiss her, then Cohen, shoving down the nerves I refuse to let build before today's practice. Just because it's the first official one as part of the team doesn't mean it needs to be any different from any other practice I've been to.

Right?

～

*I*'m still trying to convince myself that today's no big deal when I walk into the locker room, but there's something about putting your gear in your locker for the first time.

It's a sacred space.

A sense of accomplishment hits me hard.

One that means I've made it this far.

It's hard not to get choked up when I run my finger across the gold plate above my locker with KINGSTON embossed on it and my jersey hanging inside. A nervous energy I haven't felt in years kicks in.

"You ready for this, rookie?" Connor shuts his locker and turns to me.

Am I ready for this?

"You better fucking believe I'm ready," I tell him and grab my stick before turning around.

Coach O'Doul steps into the room with my brother Max beside him.

O'Doul has the presence of a hockey god, one who's played in the big games and won. And as of last May, one who's also coached and won the big game. "Good to see everyone after a few months away. I hope you all got the rest you needed and everyone enjoyed their week with the cup because as of today, last season is officially over. *Today*, we start working for our next win. What we accomplished last year has no bearing on what we do during the next eighty-two games." He crosses his thick arms over his chest and stands in the middle of the room, legs spread and his face set.

"As of today, nobody cares what you've done. We don't care how many goals you've scored, or how many games you've played. They're all going to be gunning for us. Everyone wants those bragging rights. They wanna say they beat the champs. They want to say it was a fluke that we'll never manage again. Don't give them the chance. We need to be the standard by which everyone else measures themselves. Give me everything you've got, and we'll be battling it out in the trenches again next May"—his face softens momentarily, a resigned look in his eyes—"for what'll hopefully be my last championship season."

Murmurs filter through the team until Connor takes a step forward. "You leaving us, Coach?"

O'Doul waits a beat, looking over at Max and his assistant, Quinn, whose also O'Doul's oldest daughter. She nods gently, like she's giving him courage, before he turns back to us. "I've been promising my wife I'd retire for the past ten years, and every year I tell her *just one more season*. Well, this is that season. It's time." Coach chokes up for a second before pushing it away and points his clipboard toward the team. "But if you think this means I'm gonna go easy on you—think again. My expectations are higher now than ever before. I expect this to be the best season the Philadelphia Revolution has ever had."

Sticks bang against the floor as the team chants in sync, sounding like a group of Spartan warriors readying for their general's command. It's hard to miss the way Coach chokes up.

Max steps up and shakes Coach's hand. "It's great to see everyone back this year, and while we're all going to be sad to see Coach go after this season, we've got a hell of a fight in front of us before that happens." He looks around at each of us as the locker room quiets, each player tuned in to what he's saying.

Max has always been a great public speaker. Something about my brother demands your attention before he ever opens his mouth.

Now if the fucker would only try listening every now and then, we'd be set.

"We've been kicking off the season with a team party for the past few years, and my wife and I would like to extend an invitation to you and your families to our home next Saturday night."

Quinn moves around the room, handing out red-foiled invitations with the team logo front and center. She asks each of us for an RSVP and head count as Max continues talking about the Revolution traditions and expectations. When she hands me my invite, she marks me down for two without asking, and I stop her. "Three."

"Oh," she teases. This woman is not only Max's assistant and O'Doul's daughter, but she's also my sister-in-law Wren's best friend. Which means she treats me like a little brother too. Because that's just what I need. Another fucking sibling. "And is your third anyone special?"

Damn right, she is.

~

$\mathcal{E}$very muscle in my body hurts like a fucking bitch when I walk out of the locker room after practice.

Today was long.

So. Fucking. Long.

We met with the team doctors for evaluations, then broke down into groups for time on the ice. Sprinting. Overbacks. Wallies. Every form of conditioning coaches like to threaten you with . . . O'Doul made us do.

He wanted to see who spent their summer fat, drunk, and happy.

Thank fuck that wasn't me.

"Time to separate the boys from the men," he yelled before he blew his whistle again and again. I'm not sure how many guys puked on the ice. I know there were at least two, because one of them was next to me.

Pretty sure that was the point. A true *shovel practice*. Because if you get his ice dirty, you better be ready to shovel it up.

And *okay*, I might not have puked, but even an ice bath didn't soothe my burning quads after we were done.

Walker shoulders past me, pissed as usual. "Still not impressed, rookie."

"Good thing I don't give a shit what you think, Walker."

He flips me the bird and walks out the door into the parking lot as Max calls out.

"Jace. Wait."

"Single syllables, brother?" I ask when I move around him, not in the mood to deal with his shit today.

"Jesus Christ, Jace. Just stop for a minute." He catches up to me with an annoyed glare. "You can't still actually be pissed."

"Why? Because you say I can't? Listen, Max. I don't have time to do this again. I have somewhere I need to be." Carl and Atlas will be at my house when I get home at this rate.

"You're acting like a child." And there it is. His go-to insult.

"And *you're* acting like an asshole. I get that it's your world and the rest of us are expected to bow down, but I'm telling you I'm done bowing."

"Done how? You can't be done. You signed a contract." I can't knock the smug smile from his face, can I? Where's Amelia telling me not to do it when I need her?

"Of course, you'd think I was talking about the team. I'm talking about us. You and me. You might own my hockey career for the next five years, but you don't own me, Maximus. No matter how much you pay."

"Jace, we've got to talk about this."

I shake my head. "Yeah. Maybe the next time we do that, you'll try listening. Let me know when that's on the table, and I'm there. But until then, you can save your breath, *brother*."

∼

*T*he sweet and tangy scent of BBQ greets me when I open my front door. Okay, so I didn't exactly make it home by six, but in my defense, I wanted to get her flowers. That's a good reason to be late, right?

Indy's nervous laughter is like a homing beacon calling me to her. My girl has so many different laughs. A nervous one. A shy, unsure one that's a little quieter. A loud belly laugh when Cohen does something she thinks is funny. She even has a different one when she forces a laugh at one of my jokes. Yeah . . . she doesn't always find me funny, but she hasn't told me that yet.

When I find her in the kitchen, she's shoving a serving tray at a guy I'm guessing is her brother. "Don't be a dick, Atlas. Or at least not more of a dick than you've already been."

"Come on, Indy. Nate didn't have anything going on this weekend and decided to come home with me. How does that make me a dick?"

Who the fuck is Nate?

"Not cool." Another shove of the tray. "You knew you were meeting Jace today, and that tonight was important to me. And you knew Nate's been asking me out for two years. He didn't need to be here for this."

I should focus on tonight being important to her, but I'm stuck on this Nate guy asking her out. Not gonna go over well when we meet.

"Yeah, I got it." Atlas still doesn't take the tray from her hands. "What I don't know is whether this new guy is good enough for you. Come on . . . he moved you into his house. He pays you to take care of his kid. And now what? You're dating? Fucking?"

Oh hell no.

Like a bull, I see red and charge.

169

Without another thought, I grab him by the front of his shirt and slam him against the wall.

"Jace," Indy screams and tugs at my arm. "Don't break him. He's stupid but not usually mean."

"Yeah, Jace," Atlas mutters through gritted teeth. "Listen to your employee."

"Apologize to your sister." I tighten my grip on his throat, fueled by adrenaline and anger. "I don't give a fuck who you are. You do not speak to her like that."

He fights against my hold, but I've got rage on my side.

"What the hell is going on in here?" Carl walks through the open French doors into the kitchen and looks between Indy, Atlas, and me, then takes the tray out of Indy's hand and kisses her cheek. "You know what? Forget I asked." He moves next to me and huffs. "Hope you brought your appetite. Dinner's ready."

"That's it? You're not going to tell him to get off me?" Atlas bitches.

"Son, you're in *his* house. He's got you up against a wall, and your sister's not losing her shit. Safe to say you fucked up. Now, apologize so we can have a nice dinner before hockey boy here kicks your ass."

"Like he could."

I'll admit, Atlas is a big guy. My height but a little heavier. Meatier. Definitely a football player's build. But he's got no chance on me. Not when he just hurt my girl.

"You gonna apologize to your sister?" I ask.

Carl stops with one foot out the door. "Atlas?"

"Shit," Atlas mumbles, losing his bravado.

"It's fine, Gramps, really," Indy tries to placate him.

With one look from his grandfather, any fight Atlas had deflates. "Sorry, Indy. I can't help that I'm protective of you." He looks from her to me. "And I don't know you."

"Shame I can't say it's nice to meet you. Consider this a

warning. You ever imply I'm paying her for anything other than taking care of my son again, and you'll be eating out of a straw for the foreseeable future." I let go of him and turn to her. "You okay?"

She nods gently.

I bend and pick up the flowers I dropped when I walked into this shit show. "Got these for you, pretty girl."

"Fucking gross." Atlas scrunches up his face, like Cohen does when he's blowing out his diaper, and groans. "Dude, I'm right here."

Indy purses her lips, less than impressed. "He's not the one who just implied I was sleeping with my boss for money like a whore, you shit." She shoves his shoulder and brushes past him to join her grandfather outside, leaving the two of us alone in the awkward as hell silence.

"So . . ." Atlas sizes me up, probably trying to decide whether or not he could take me.

Newsflash.

He can't.

"What are your intentions with my sister?"

"You're kidding, right?" I laugh. "She's incredible, and she deserves better than the way you just treated her. Listen, I've got sisters, so I get it. Be grateful your sister isn't as violent as mine are. They would have ripped my balls off and fed them to the dog if I said what you did."

"Just don't fuck her over, okay? She deserves better than that. If anyone ever deserved the fucking fairytale, it's Indy."

And I'm going to make sure she gets it.

171

# INDIA

"**S**o Jace, when's your first game?" Gramps asks across from the table as Atlas and Nate do the dishes inside. Gramps declared that since we hosted and he cooked, they had to clean. Totally fair, if you ask me.

"We've got our first preseason game in two weeks. I can get you tickets if you'd like to come, sir."

I roll my lips in, trying not to laugh when he calls Gramps *sir*. I'd say he's laying it on thick, but I know my grandfather is sure to love it. "You should come, Gramps. You could explain what's happening to me."

"Are you going to bring your knitting needles with you? You know you're not going to watch the game. At least you never did when I had it on the TV," Gramps calls me out.

My skin heats when thoughts of the last time I saw Jace on skates flash through my mind. "I think it's going to be a little more interesting, now that I know a few of the players."

"A few?" Jace asks, clearly not liking my answers.

"You didn't think it was just you, did you, hockey boy?" Gramps taunts, and Jace's mouth opens and closes a few times like a fish.

"You're damn right, I did," he finally says to me, not Gramps, then relaxes when I laugh.

"Only you, handsome." I press a kiss to Jace's cheek.

"What the fuck?" Atlas groans when he sits back down. "Do we have to watch you kiss at the dinner table?"

Nate, thankfully, is smart enough to stay quiet.

Gramps, however, doesn't feel the need. "Son, you don't have to watch anything. You have a car and an apartment three hours from here. When it's your house, you make the rules."

"Whatever. I guess it could be worse." Atlas smiles like he's up to something. "So tell me, Kingston. Are you going to marry my sister?"

"Atlas!" I snap.

"Yes," Jace answers just as quickly.

"Excuse me?" Gramps glares.

"Guess I'm not getting that date now, huh?" Nate adds, and we all answer at once.

"No."

⁓

"Thanks for coming." I wave, slightly deranged, as Gramps and Atlas pull away in their trucks. Once they're out of site, I give up the calm facade I've been clinging to since the whole marriage discussion and try to get my bearings.

I close my eyes and lean my head back against the door, attempting to catch my breath when Jace's voice filters down to me from Cohen's room, crooning a different Foo Fighters song tonight to soothe the sweet boy.

So much for catching my breath.

I flip the lock and head upstairs, my heart racing in an entirely different way, when I stop in front of Cohen's open door and find Jace, shirtless, with Cohen asleep on his chest. This man . . . His sexy smile slips into place when he sees me. "Hey, pretty girl," he whispers.

"Hey." I move into the room and peel the baby from his chest. My fingers brush against his hot skin, and I swear my blood ignites. "You wanna know a secret?" I ask softly as I place Cohen down in his bassinet.

Jace steps up behind me, his hands moving to my hips and his dick hard against my ass. "I want to know all your secrets, baby."

I look over my shoulder and lick my lips. "So many versions of you turn me on, Jace Kingston." I turn around and press my hands against his chest, moving him backward. "The possessive, protective version from earlier turns me on."

I maneuver us out of Cohen's room. "The sweet, sexy side you like to save for when no one else is around."

And as I back him into his bedroom, I whisper against his lips, "But my favorite version of you . . . the one that might as well incinerate my panties on the spot, is you"—I nip his bottom lip and unsnap the top button of his jeans—"in daddy mode."

I make quick work of his zipper before he grabs my hands. "Do you have a daddy kink you're hiding from me, Indy?"

"No," I pull my shirt over my head and drop it to the floor, enjoying the way Jace's pupils blow wide with need. "I have a *you* kink."

"Correct fucking answer, pretty girl." He tosses me onto the bed, then yanks my pants and thong down in a smooth move, then smacks my ass cheek. "Now get on your knees and get that ass in the air."

I unhook my bra and toss it at him, then hurry to my knees and look back at Jace. His muscles bunch as he shoves

175

his jeans and boxers down and kicks them to the floor. Jace places a knee on the bed and kisses his way up my spine. "Good girl."

Then he rubs his cock through my center, and I hum, loving the feel of his big body behind me. "Do you want me to get a condom?"

I shake my head. "No. I want to feel you."

"You like that," Jace growls against my skin as he smacks my clit with his swollen cock. "You want my cock, pretty girl?"

My forehead falls to the bed as he teases my pussy, dragging the head of his cock through my soaked sex until I'm teetering on the edge of sanity, unsure how much more I can take. Panting and moaning and desperate for more. "Jase . . . stop teasing me."

"You want me to fuck that perfect cunt, Indy?" I moan, and he wraps my hair around his fist and tugs when I don't answer. "What was that?"

"Yes, please," I pant. "Fuck me." I push back against him, desperate for friction, dying for him.

He pulls me up and runs his lips along my jaw, then pushes his tongue inside my mouth as he pushes into me. With each achingly slow stroke, my body relaxes around him. Dying to take him deeper. Begging to get him closer.

His callused fingers grip my jaw, and our tongues move in a ruthless harmony until he finally presses all the way in. A savage cry catches in my throat.

"Don't scream, pretty girl." He reaches around and plays with my clit until I'm utterly consumed. Overwhelmed but wanting more. His lips skim my ear as he whispers, "If you scream, this stops."

I loop my arm back around his neck and bring my lips to his as he sets a punishing rhythm with every hard, brutal snap of his hips. Bruisingly. Giving me exactly what I need before I even know to ask for it. Reading my body perfectly. "Oh God," I gasp, my breath thready and lost. "Jace."

"I'm right here with you." He pinches my clit. "Let go, Indy."

I clench around him as my toes curl and my body shakes.

Jace wraps his arms around my chest and holds me tightly to him as he jerks and comes inside me, both of us gasping for breath as we come down from our high. "Jesus, Indy."

I drop my head back against his chest, trying to catch my breath. "Me too, Jace."

Me too.

# JACE

*T*he following Friday, Boone is spotting me in the weight room as we finish up the lifting part of our day. Coach O'Doul split us up into groups at the beginning of the week. Half lift before practice, the other half lift after.

Today's our *after* day.

I fucking hate *after* days.

And *after* day, when it's *leg* day, is the absolute fucking worst.

"You bringing that family of yours to the kickoff party at your brother's place this weekend?" Boone finishes his last rep and rests the bar back on the squat rack, then stretches out his quads.

We swap places, and I roll my shoulders, then get under the bar, bend my knees, and step out from the rack. "I really don't want to go to this thing. But yes, I'm bringing Indy and Cohen with me. With any luck Cohen will puke all over Max, and I can leave early."

"There's something I've been meaning to ask you. What's the deal with that southern belle friend of hers? She's smokin hot, and you know what they say about redheads."

"Harper?" I push through my last rep, then answer him, "I don't know her very well yet. But Harper, Sophie, and Indie are thick as thieves. You want me to ask Indy to invite them to the game next week?"

We switch places again. "Yeah, rookie. You should invite them. Let 'em see us crush the Penguins."

Connor gets off the bench behind us and laughs at Boone. "You done with the puck bunnies so soon, man? I figured you still had a few more years of them in you."

Boone grunts through his last set. "I don't know, Cap. Rookie here makes the settled thing look good."

I shrug. "I make *everything* look good."

"You bringing anybody this weekend, Cap?" Boone asks.

"It's not a wedding, shithead. It's players and *families*. You're not supposed to bring a first date to the kickoff party."

"Come on, Cap. You need to loosen up and get laid." Boone and I follow Connor out of the weight room. "Maybe not in that order."

"*You* need to grow up and find a new place to live. Maybe then you'd be . . ." Smoke looks like it's about to blow out of Connor's ears. "Nope. You'd still be a dick."

I ignore them when my phone vibrates and pull it out of my shorts. That's when I see my private investigator's number flashing across the screen. "Hello?"

"Mr. Kingston, this is Mr. Scavo's office. Are you available to come downtown this afternoon for a meeting? Mr. Scavo has some information to discuss with you. We've found your son's mother."

Holy shit.

My heart threatens to beat out of my chest.

So many fucking scenarios run through my brain.

"I'll be there in twenty minutes."

"*I*t looks like your daddy beat us home, little man," I hear Indy telling Cohen as she walks through the house into the kitchen, where I've been sitting and nursing a bottle of bourbon for hours.

"Hi . . ." Her eyes bounce between me and the crystal glass of amber liquid. "Are you okay?"

She walks to me, and I pull Cohen and her down on my lap, burying my face in her hair. God, she smells good. "I am, now that you're home. Where were you guys?"

"We met Harper and Sophie for cupcakes and coffee at Sweet Temptations, then popped in to say hi to Gramps and Gladys at The Bee." Her voice gets sugary sweet after she kisses Cohen's head the way she just kissed mine. "And now it's time for our little man's dinner."

I take Cohen from her and rest him against my shoulder. "Hear that, buddy? Pretty sure she's claiming you too."

"Why should you have all the fun?" She turns on my lap, laying one hand on Cohen's back and wrapping the other one around my neck. "You're not the only one who gets to do the claiming, Kingston." Her mouth ghosts across my lips. "You're mine, Jace. Both you and Cohen. And I'm not letting either one of you go."

"You promise, pretty girl?" My voice cracks as I ask through the emotion clogging my throat.

"Jace . . . what's going on?"

I run my fingers through her silky hair, unable to speak for a minute. "I met with the private investigator earlier. He found her."

"Found—" Her eyes soften. "Oh. *Her.*"

She firms her grip on Cohen. "She can't have him," she argues. "She left him. No court is going to give him back to her now. They can't, Jace. They can't take him away from us."

"Indy . . ." I stare into the liquid gold of her tear-filled eyes.

"I'll be right there with you every single step of this fight. She can't have him back. Not him and not you."

"That's the thing." I blow out my breath, trying to hold down the bile forcing its way up my throat. "She isn't coming after Cohen."

"She's not?" Indy asks in disbelief because nothing is ever that fucking simple. Her body tightens, readying for a fight.

"No, baby." A cold sweat breaks out over my skin as acid churns in my stomach. "She's dead, Indy. She OD'd five days after Cohen was born."

"Oh, Jace. I'm so sorry." She presses her forehead to mine, and I close my eyes. "Did you get any answers? Like who she was? Why she didn't want to be involved in Cohen's life?" She rises from my lap and runs her hand over Cohen's back. "How could she leave him?"

The next wave of pain hits. "Her name was Allison. She was a puck bunny I slept with last fall. She went to a school in Connecticut. Eventually, she started dating my roommate, Sean, but I swear to God, I had no idea she was pregnant."

"Did your roommate know? I mean, she must have been showing last semester."

"Neither of them ever said a thing." There's no good way to tell her this. "They broke up in February, and she wasn't showing then."

Indy paces around the kitchen, attempting to burn off whatever nervous energy she can. "Have you talked to your roommate yet? Maybe he can fill in some blanks."

"He and I don't talk." I stand up and buckle Cohen into the swing in the corner of the kitchen, then turn and wrap my arms around Indy. "I already told you I've done some things I'm not proud of. And what happened with Sean was probably the worst of it."

"You don't have to tell me, Jace."

"But I do . . . I told you before I wasn't proud of the guy I was last year. What I didn't tell you was how out of control I was. I'd wake up, smoke a joint like most people brush their teeth and follow it with a shot like it was no big deal. I never showed up to class sober. I'd become so damn good at hiding it, nobody knew. It was easier to not feel anything that way." I bury my face in her hair, not wanting to look at her and see the disgust I know will be in her eyes. "I hit rock bottom the night I slept with Allison and Sean's sister last February. I got so fucked up, I didn't even remember doing it when I woke up."

"Jace." She steps out of my hold.

"You've gotta believe me. If I'd known. If I had any fucking clue, I'd have taken care of her. Would have made sure she was okay. Would have been there for the doctor's appointments and the day he was born. I'd have been there for her *after* . . ." I drop to my knees and wrap my arms around her waist. "That night changed everything. I got my shit together after that. You've got to believe me."

She drops down to her knees in front of me, fat tears clinging to her long lashes, and grabs my hands in hers. "Of course I believe you, Jace. We all make mistakes. It's what we do afterward that matters."

She presses her lips tenderly against mine. "And you, Jace Kingston, might have had some issues to work through, but you've done it. And the man I know . . ." Another kiss. "You're a good man. A good father. She didn't want you to know before he was born, Jace. She could have told you, and she *chose* not to. We may never know her reason, but she knew you'd be a great dad because she *chose* to have Cohen here when she could have gone to any other hospital. You said it yourself, she didn't even live in Kroydon Hills. Then she *chose* to put your name on his birth certificate when she could

183

have left it blank. I'm sorry she'll never get to know Cohen because our sweet boy is going to be an incredible man one day, just like his father. But she made her choices, and you've made yours. And that little boy is going to have an amazing life because of those choices."

I never knew words could hit so fucking hard.

*Our sweet boy.*

I rest my chin on the top of her head and breathe her in. "Our sweet boy, Indy. Yours and mine."

And I'm never letting go of either one of them.

# INDIA

*G*rowing up, I loved that old Julia Roberts movie —*Pretty Woman*. Not that I ever fantasized about being a hooker or anything, but the idea of a gorgeous man coming in to sweep me off my feet . . . that was the fantasy. However, the reality of being the poor girl on the arm of the rich guy at a fancy event isn't quite the fairytale I fantasized it would be. There's no brown polka-dot dress and wide-brimmed hat. But when I met up with Harper and Sophie yesterday, Harper handed me a garment bag with three different sundresses in it and a cute pair of wedges that went with all three. She said I needed something new for the kickoff party at Jace's brother's house today, and *wow*, was she right.

The women here look like they've been buffed, blown-out, and air-brushed to within an inch of their lives. They're beautiful and sophisticated, and even though I feel way out of my league, I don't think you can tell at first glance. I settled on a butter-yellow strapless maxi-dress that swooshes around my ankles.

It's sweet and summery and hides my scar completely.

*Baby steps.*

The yard is filled with players and their families. Waiters wearing white gloves walk around with hors d'oeuvres and drinks to entertain the adults. While a bounce house and a clown making balloon animals sit off to the side of the resort-worthy pool, next to an ice cream truck and hot dog stand.

Jace introduces me to his teammates and their wives, who all seem nice but so far out of my comfort zone, and I breathe a sigh of relief when we finally talk to Boone and Connor.

Eventually, Jace's big palm slides to the small of my back, and he moves me out of the way as a tiny toddler in a pink gingham romper runs to her Uncle Jace. I think I recognize her from the Kings game. A thought that's confirmed a moment later when Jace's sister-in-law Daphne takes the little girl's hand in hers. "Hi, guys." Daphne smiles, genuinely happy. "I'm so glad you could make it today."

Jace leans in and kisses them both, then watches as they fawn over Cohen.

Unfortunately, that means he misses his brother walking our way. Max Kingston is incredibly handsome. A little blonder and a tiny bit shorter than his youngest brother. But the family resemblance is uncanny. His navy-blue eyes rest on his wife and daughter at first in relaxed contentment. But I don't miss the tightness that takes over his face when he looks at Jace and Cohen.

Daphne reaches out, taking Cohen from him, then winks at me. "Come on, Indy. How about you let me show you around?"

I look around our small group, unsure whether to go with her or stay with Jace until he kisses my forehead. "Go ahead. I'll find you in a few minutes."

Daphne pats Serena's back and tells her to go play as we

walk away. "Thanks so much for coming with me. I've been trying to get those two to talk all summer without any luck. I thought for sure they'd work things out by now, but they're both so damn stubborn."

My hackles rise.

I know she's Jace's sister-in-law, but I don't love hearing her call him stubborn.

Even if I know how stubborn he is.

We walk through the beautifully manicured yard, around the bounce house and pool, then into the house, where a waiter hands us each a glass of lemonade. "Your home is lovely," I tell Daphne as I take it all in.

"Thank you." She sits down at the table, primly crosses her legs, and pats Cohen's back. "Now spill."

I choke on my lemonade and look through the windows at Jace and Max. "Excuse me?"

Hudson and his wife, Maddie, join us a moment later as I try to stop coughing. Maddie takes the seat next to me. "Are you okay, Indy?"

"Yes," I croak. "Just fine."

"Hud, how about you leave us ladies alone for a few?" Maddie asks her husband.

"But I want to hear the gossip too," Hudson whines like a little kid.

"And I'll tell you later," she tells him through gritted teeth. "Go."

Daphne giggles, and the three of us watch world heavyweight MMA Champion, Hudson Kingston, walk away, having been bested by his teeny-tiny wife. Once he's out of sight, we all turn back to the table before both women set their sights on me. Daphne settles Cohen in the crook of her arm and smiles. "Now, Indy, are you ready to help me?"

Maddie's eyes brighten with excitement. "Oh, this sounds juicy. What are you two up to?"

"Nothing," I announce a little too loudly. "Daphne and I just left Max and Jace—"

"Say no more." She leans her elbows on the table and rests her face in her hands. "Does this little operation get the guys to talk again? Because the family dinners have seriously sucked all summer with those two avoiding each other at all costs."

Daphne pushes a plate of baby quiches my way, then Maddie pops one into her mouth. "So how do we fix it?"

"We chew first, Mads." Daphne grins.

"Whatever, D. I'm tired of the tension. And if the guys aren't going to get their shit together, you two will have to help them."

"It looks like both of you have this under control. So there's no need for me." I rise from the chair before the matching glares on both their faces forces me back down. "Okay, fine. What do I need to do?"

"Uhm . . . ladies?" The three of us turn our heads to find Connor coming toward us. "I hate to interrupt you, but Jace and Max look like they're about to come to blows."

"Blows?" I jump up. "Like a fistfight?" Oh shit.

"Relax," Maddie tells us. "Hudson's out there. He won't let them get into a fight."

"I'm sorry." I stand and take Cohen back from Daphne in case we need to make a quick exit. "Jace has had a really bad weekend already, and he doesn't need this today."

"Is he okay?" Daphne asks.

"I'm not sure," I tell her honestly.

It's not my story to tell, but I think it's time for us to go.

∽

*J*ace

"I don't want to do this, Max. Not here."

He glares back at me like a bug that just ruined his car's brand-new wax job. "You've refused to talk to me every time I've tried. This is getting ridiculous, and you're not leaving me a ton of options, Jace."

Groaning, I glance over to see Coach O'Doul watching us and lower my voice. "You can talk as much as you want, Maximus. But it doesn't mean I have to get over anything."

"You always were good at fucking everything up, then throwing a fit until you got your way. I guess some things never change." He hits his mark hard. Family always knows just how to make it hurt. "But here's the thing, little brother . . . I'm not sure what the hell would make you happy. Do you even know anymore?"

"Only you would be so fucking arrogant, brother. You want to know what I want? I want to wipe that smug fucking grin off your face." I close the distance between Max and me, then see Hudson out of the corner of my eye before he jumps between us.

"*Family* party, remember, guys?"

"I'm just saying." Max looks around the party, pasting a fake as fuck smile on his face and lowering his voice. "It looks like staying in Kroydon Hills worked out for you, after all. You've got your family around to help with Cohen. And rumor has it, things are heating up between you and Indy. Maybe you should try being a little grateful for what you've been given, instead of resenting how easy it was."

My fists clench at my sides.

"Oh right. You don't know the meaning of the word."

That's it. My vision tunnels, and I see red.

I don't think before I swing on my brother. It's something I've wanted to do for months. But the reality of actually hitting him crashes down on me the second I hear the crunch.

I just hit my oldest brother.

Max fucking Kingston.

Owner of the Revolution.

In front of the entire team.

Max takes the hit, then smiles as he cups his jaw. "Look at you, growing a set of balls. Maybe there's still hope after all."

"I'll show you fucking hope, asshole." Hudson jumps between us, banding an arm around my chest when he sees me ready to swing again. "Fuck you, Max. I'll play for you, *brother*. But that's it. I meant what I said before. I'm done."

Max's hand comes up to cradle his jaw as Daphne runs over to him with Indy trailing behind. "What the hell, Jace?" Daphne shrieks.

"Go home, Jace. I'll handle this." Hudson shoves me back, blocking my path to Max.

"Like I need to be handled, asshole," Max fumes behind him. "You've been handed everything your entire life, Jace. You don't get to resent it now."

"People are watching you," my sister-in-law hisses, and my brother instantly transforms from the pissed-off head of the family to the happy host of today's party.

Indy tucks herself into my side with Cohen on her shoulder, and I wrap an arm around them. "We're leaving."

~

*W*hen Indy and I walk in the door ten minutes later, I go straight to the kitchen and stare at the bottle of bourbon from yesterday. Ready to forget the last thirty-six hours. At least for a little while.

"Jace . . ." Indy whispers as she moves in front of me, blocking my view. "Do you want to talk about it?"

"No." I wrap my fingers in the soft hair at the nape of her neck and tug. "I don't think I can talk tonight."

She eyes the bourbon on the counter, and a mix of worry and disappointment flashes in her eyes. "Okay. Then I'll give Cohen his bottle and put him to bed while you pour yourself a drink."

I don't miss the disdain lacing her words.

She's right.

Alcohol isn't the answer to this fucking day.

I open the bottle and pour the rest of it down the sink, then turn back to her and take Cohen. "How about you let me do it?"

She nods, then gently runs her hand down my arm.

"Thanks for being here, pretty girl."

Her eyes grow warm. "I'm not going anywhere."

Those four words hold more weight than she'll ever know.

⁓

Once I get Cohen changed into his pajamas with the little paw prints embroidered on the bottoms of his feet, we settle into the rocker with his bottle, and both our eyes get heavy as he drinks. My buddy is sound asleep before he even finishes the last drop, but I don't put him to bed right away. Instead, we rock in the chair while I replay the last twenty-four hours, wondering when my life turned into a fucking dumpster fire.

Any work I've done to distance myself from being the Kingston on the team went down in flames today. Max and I have had a rough relationship since he became my legal guardian, but I never thought it would come to this. Not when I was fifteen and Dad died. And definitely not now, when I'm a grown fucking man.

I'm not sure how much time has passed when Indy pads softly into Cohen's room.

"Jace . . ." she whispers quietly as she takes Cohen from my chest.

He tips his little face up to the ceiling, pursing his lips together and bending his knees, pulling them up against his chest like a tight little ball. A perfect little prince. That's what they always called us as kids, little princes and princesses. I used to hate it. It's only now, as I look at my son, that I get it.

The feeling that your kid is the most special thing in the world.

It's followed by an overwhelming fear I'm going to fuck him up.

After she lays him down in his bassinet, Indy steps between my legs. "Are you okay, handsome? You were quiet all night."

I run my hands over her hips, bunching the soft fabric in my hands. "I don't deserve you, pretty girl."

"Why would you say that?" Her eyes search mine.

"Because I'm probably gonna fuck this up the way I've fucked up everything else, and I don't want to hurt you."

"Then don't hurt me." She laces her fingers through mine, then tugs me up. "And don't you dare say you don't deserve me, because I'm pretty sure you're the universe's way of rewarding me for going through hell."

I stand and cup her face in my hands. "I hit my brother tonight."

"You did." She presses her lips against the palm of my hand. "Do you want to talk about it?"

I shake my head and lead her out of the room and into the hall. "No. I don't want to talk."

She leans back against the floor-to-ceiling window overlooking the falls below and circles an arm around my neck. "Then let's not talk."

She presses her soft lips to my neck . Shivers race down my spine at the contact, and I pick her up, wrapping both her legs around my waist.

"Be with me," she whispers breathlessly as her heated breath skims along my jaw.

I capture her mouth in a scorching kiss, sweeping my tongue against hers. Tasting. Teasing. Drowning in this woman I'll never deserve. Letting her anchor me to the life I've grown to love. My hand slides up the soft skin of her creamy thighs, hidden under the layers of yellow fabric like a present waiting to be opened.

My present.

A sharp sweet gasp pushes past her lips when my thumb skims her hot sex through the rough lace of her panties.

"Do you like that, baby?" I drag my tongue along the golden skin of her bare shoulders, my cock already hard and desperate for her.

She moans again and jerks my belt free before she shoves her hands down the front of my pants. My cock leaks in her hands, begging for her touch. Needing to be buried inside her.

Indy rolls her thumb through the precum, then sucks it between her lips with a triumphant grin.

"Fuck, Indy," I growl as I shove her panties to the side and, in one powerful thrust, push inside her tight cunt.

We both freeze as Indy's breath catches in her throat, her body adjusting to mine.

So fucking tight.

So fucking hot.

So fucking mine.

"You're fucking dripping for me, pretty girl."

She clings to me with glassy eyes. "You feel so good, Jace," she pants. "So good. Please move." Her shoes dangle from her toes before she kicks them to the floor. She clings to me, pressing her chest firmly to mine, digging her heels into my ass and hoisting herself higher to get the angle she needs. To take what she wants.

Indy grinds down on my cock, and I groan, "That's it, baby. You take my cock like such a good girl."

I yank down her strapless dress and bare the most perfect breasts I've ever seen. High and tight. Pale skin and pretty pink nipples begging to be sucked and licked and bitten. I press my lips to the scar buried in the valley between her breasts, kissing her reverently before I drag one hard nipple between my teeth until she's panting and taking what she wants from me. Begging me for more.

With my arms wrapped around her waist, I pull out slowly, then push back in over and over in lazy thrust after lazy thrust. Taking my time. Savoring each gasp, each whisper.

The connection between us more intense than it's ever been.

With her eyes fixed on mine, Indy's mouth opens, a silent plea on her lips as she tenses around me.

I capture her lips in mine swallowing her moans as she arches her back shaking in my arms. She throws her head back, and a raw, beautiful moan pours from her lips as her pussy milks me for every last drop.

A white-hot heat catches at the base of my spine, ripping through me, and I grip the globes of her ass in both hands and fuck inside her one last time.

"You were made for me, Indy."

"Don't let go, Jace." She drops her head to mine and closes her eyes.

"Never, baby."

# INDIA

*J* reach across the bed Monday morning, expecting to find Jace lying next to me, but come up empty when my hand runs over cool sheets where Jace should be. Instead I bury my face in his pillow and close my eyes. Maybe just a few more minutes.

"Good morning, pretty girl."

"Morning," I tell him from under his blankets. "Why are you so far away?"

"Game days always amp me up. I needed to burn some energy."

I grab his t-shirt from the foot of the bed and throw it on, unwilling to be so far away. Padding gently across the room, I wrap my arms around his waist. "I can think of a better way to burn off excess energy, handsome." I press my cheek to his bare back, my fingertips running along his warm abs.

"I figured I'd take advantage of the quiet and get this done." He turns his head toward me and presses a kiss to my lips. Soft and tender, it holds a promise for later.

I look over his shoulder and see a pile of shirts sitting on the dresser. "What are you doing? Rearranging your drawers?"

"I'm making room for you. You sleep in here every night. It doesn't make sense for all your stuff to be in a different room." He says this so nonchalantly, like he didn't just decide I was moving into his room without talking to me about it.

Warning bells play an almost furious symphony in my head, and my brother's voice narrates them.

*He's paying you, Indy.*

*You're in his house and his life because you're paid to be here.*

*This isn't a relationship. It's employment.*

"Jace." I drop my arms and stare in disbelief. "Why would I move my things in here?"

"What do you mean *why*? We live together. We sleep together. We're raising Cohen together. Doesn't it make sense that we'd share a room?" He looks genuinely confused, and I suddenly think I might hyperventilate.

"Oh." The room suddenly gets hot and starts to close in on me.

"What's wrong, baby?" He wraps a lock of my hair around his finger. "I thought you'd be happy. It's not a big deal. I've got more room than I need."

I take a step back, needing a clear head that I most certainly won't get with him touching me. "Did you even hear what you just said?" *Oh God.* "We live together *because I work for you*. We're raising Cohen together *because I work for you*. We've skipped over so many steps, Jace. I'm not Cohen's mother. I'm not your wife. We're not playing house. We've fallen into this thing really fast. And now you're just assuming I'm going to move into your room without even talking to me."

Fear scratches at me, yanking me down by its long, wrinkly fingers.

Fighting to keep me in its grasp.

Smothering me until I can't breathe.

The confusion on his face mixes with hurt, and together they pack a punch that hits harder than the one he threw at the party. "I don't get it. If you don't want to share a room, we don't have to. It just seemed easier."

"I guess that's the thing. Everything has been so easy for us." An almost silent sob pushes past my lips. We've just sort of fallen into this place. We didn't work for it. We didn't date. We didn't take it slow, even though I knew we needed to."

"Indy . . ." He reaches for me.

"No, Jace. I don't want to just settle for this life because it's easy."

"Settle? You're *settling* with us?" Anger replaces his earlier confusion and sucks all the air from my lungs.

"No. That's not what I meant," I tell him through trembling lips. "I'm saying this is all wrong."

"Or maybe you're finally saying what you actually mean." He shuts the drawer with an almost eerie calmness. "I'm so fucking tired of everyone telling me I've had it so easy and never had to work for anything. Everything has been easy with us, India, because from the minute you walked in my door, my entire fucking soul knew it found its other half. Something you obviously don't feel. I know what I mean and what I want. Why don't you think about what you meant and let me know when you figure it the fuck out."

Before I know it, he's gone, and the shower is running behind the closed bathroom door. Oh God. What just happened?

*C*ohen and I kept a low profile until Jace left for his morning practice. He's got a walkthrough today and his first preseason game tonight. Then he'll be gone for two away games.

Maybe that's a good thing.

*Maybe* we need some space.

At least, I'll have time to figure out what the hell I'm doing without him here clouding my judgment for a few days, even if my heart hurts thinking about him being gone.

Cohen and I lie on a blanket on the floor, playing with his activity mat later that morning. The French doors are open, and a warm breeze rolls in off the lake. The sweet smell of summer is fading, making way for the cool crisp air of fall. One season rolling into the next, and I can't help but wonder if that's a metaphor for Jace and me.

One season ending so another can start.

Damn it. I need some advice.

Cohen's little hand makes contact with the brightly colored mirror hanging above his face, and he squeals triumphantly.

I reach for my phone, ready to call in the reinforcements, except it rings before I can pick it up. A pang of disappointment hits when I see the unknown number flashing on the screen, part of me clinging to the hope that it's Jace. "Hello?"

"Good morning," a distinctly male voice responds. "I'm trying to reach India Monroe. This is Mr. Schenk calling from Kroydon Hills Prep School."

"Good morning." I sit up, shocked to be hearing from Mr. Schenk. "This is India.

"Hello, Miss Monroe. We interviewed you a few months ago to fill in for our first-grade teacher while she was out on maternity leave. I know that position didn't work out. However, our kindergarten position has opened up quite unexpectedly, and I'd like to offer it to you. Of course, I understand if you're no longer interested, but we're hoping you are."

"You're offering me a job?" I ask, completely shocked.

This is my dream school.

The one I've been applying to for nearly a year.

I did my student teaching at Kroydon Prep my last semester of college and have had it pinned to my vision board for ten months.

"Yes, Miss Monroe. I'm offering you a job. If you'd like to come in to discuss the details, I'm available this afternoon."

I look over at Cohen, and my heart breaks.

I can't leave him. Not even because I signed a one-year contract but because I love him, and the idea of someone else taking care of him literally hurts my heart. "I'm actually not available today, Mr. Schenk."

"I didn't think we'd be that lucky. How about I ask my assistant to email you all the information?"

"Thank you. That would be perfect. I appreciate it."

"Please understand that I need to move quickly on this position, Miss Monroe. Our board of trustees hopes to have this position filled as soon as possible."

"I understand." My heart sinks. "Thank you."

I end the call and drag my hands over my face.

"Are you going to take the job?" Jace steps into the room, scaring me.

"I didn't realize you were home." I stand, trying to calm my racing heart. This is not happening. Not now, when the timing couldn't be worse. Not when Jace and I need to talk.

"It was a walkthrough. They're fast."

"Oh." My heart drops into my stomach, and the room suddenly feels shaky.

"Is it teaching kindergarten?" He moves next to me.

"Yes," I whisper, scared each word is another nail in our

coffin. I might not know what's happening with us, but I know I don't want it to end.

"Then you have to take it. It's what you wanted. It's the dream Atlas didn't want me crushing, right?" Jace reaches out for me before he drops his hand at the last moment.

I lace my fingers through his. "I signed a one-year contract."

"Fuck the contract, Indy." He drops my hand. "If this is what you want, just go. We'll be fine without you."

I plant my feet, refusing to rock back from the force of his words. "Oh."

"Just give me the week to get someone lined up. When we get back from this stretch of away games, you can go." He bends down and picks up Cohen before he disappears from the room, and I'm left standing, frozen and broken.

How could so much go wrong so quickly?

# JACE

For most teams, game days are well-oiled machines.

An early, easy walkthrough. A light lunch.

Some guys take a nap. I usually take a nap, but that wasn't happening today.

Everyone has their own pregame rituals. Our goalie, Deacon, is carefully laying out all his gear on the floor. He's spread out, quietly getting in the zone. Everyone has warned us new guys not to touch any of his stuff. Goalies are usually one of the more superstitious guys on the team, and from what I've seen already, Deacon is the rule, not the exception.

I tape my stick with the same brand of tape I've used for ten years. I only use black tape, and it's gotta wrap around ten times. Not nine. Not eleven. Ten. After that, I'm good. I don't need silence. I don't need to get in the zone. I'm there, and I'm ready.

Connor sits down next to me, his pants and pads on and his sweater still hanging in his locker. "Why do you look like someone ran over your fucking dog, rookie?"

"I don't have a dog, Cap," I tell him as I pull the tape taunt around my blade.

"Then what's wrong with you? Because I can't decide if you're pissed or you gotta take a shit."

I rip the tape from my blade and start again. "I'm fine, man. I've just got things on my mind."

"Aww shit, man. Did you and the wife get in a fight?"

His words hit me square in the chest, and I think about my mom's engagement ring I dropped off at the jewelers Saturday morning to be reset. It wasn't like I was going to propose right away, but I wanted to have it ready for whenever the moment hit. "Yeah. I guess we did."

"What did you do wrong?"

I finish taping the blade before turning his way. "Why the fuck did I have to do something wrong?"

"Because I have four fucking sisters, shithead. The guys are always wrong."

"Who's wrong?" Boone asks as he drops down on my other side, fully dressed for the game.

"Jace fucked up with Indy."

"Ooh," Boone exaggerates. "How'd you fuck up, rookie?"

"I didn't fuck up. I was making room for her stuff in my drawers. How's that fucking up?"

"Did you ask her first?" Connor challenges.

"Yup. Girls like to be asked, not told," Boone agrees.

"How the hell would you know, asswipe? When was the last time you had a girlfriend?" Connor lobs back.

"I've watched movies, okay? You can learn a lot from Ryan Reynolds."

Connor and I ignore his boneheaded comment. "Seriously, you think she was pissed because I didn't ask? She started talking about how we missed all these steps. And how she works for me. I don't fucking know, man. Then when I came back from the walkthrough this morning, she was on the phone with some school offering her a job."

"Shit. What are you gonna do?" Boone asks while Connor shakes his head.

"No clue, man. No clue." O'Doul and Max walk into the room, and my skin fucking crawls when I feel everyone's eyes on me. The bruise on Max's jaw isn't helping matters.

"Settle down, men." Coach waits until the room quiets around him. "Feel that energy? That's first-game-of-the-year energy. New season. New mission. New teammates. Tonight's your chance to show us what you're made of. For some of you, tonight's your chance to earn your spot. For others, maybe it's the start of your swan song. I want you to go out there and play your game the way we've trained. Show me you want to be part of the Revolution. Now let's go play some hockey and have a little fun."

Max doesn't add anything.

Walker turns to me after they walk out of the room. That same disdain in place that's always there when he looks at me. "You ready for this, Kingston? You're playing with the big boys tonight. Let's see if you can hang or if you're only tough when you're taking shots at old men in suits."

"Fuck you, Walker. Max could kick your ass from here to the river and back if he wanted to." I don't bother telling him I can say and do whatever the fuck I want to my brother, but I'll be damned before I let anyone else say a word.

Connor pushes me in front of him before I fight my own team's enforcer, and we file through the tunnel and out onto the ice for a warm-up.

I do a lap around the rink, looking up into the stands, stopping when I see Lenny holding Cohen by the boards. They're both dressed in matching Kingston jerseys. Cohen has tiny custom-made noise-canceling headphones on, and like a fucking pussy, my heart pangs that Indy's not the one down here holding my son. I skate over and knock on the board until my baby looks over at me and giggles.

Lenny beams proudly through the glass. "Kick ass, little brother."

"Thanks, Len."

I wait until she's back up the stairs to stretch out, and Boone stops next to me. "Damn Kingston. She's hot."

"She's my sister, and she's married, fuck-nut." But if Cohen's here being held by Lenny, maybe Indy's here too and there's still hope.

~

## Indy

Jace's entire family came tonight to watch him play his first professional game, and my heart can barely take it when he lines up for the first puck drop. I'm standing in the Kingston's box, sandwiched between Gramps and Harper. Sophie had a class she couldn't skip, but we've sent some pictures to our group chat, so she can be with us in spirit.

Not that she'd want my poor pathetic spirit tonight.

"Do you know what's happening?" Harper asks with excited eyes as she sips her wine, and I shake my head.

"Not really," I tell her with a happy Cohen tucked in my arms. Tiny custom headphones cover his ears because unlike the suites at the football stadium, this box isn't soundproof.

Jace skates down the ice, going for the puck and gets slammed into the corner behind the goal. "Oh my God." I hold my breath.

Lenny leans over me and points. "Now watch how he comes out of the corner with the puck though. Jace is merciless."

True to Lenny's word, he emerges from the corner with

control of the puck, then passes to Connor, who shoots. The puck rockets right around the goalie's leg, and he dives for it. And oh my God, he scored. The red light behind the goal flashes, and the arena erupts.

I cheer too, then look at Cohen, who's just smiling while taking it all in.

Guess the headphones work.

"How many times did I try to get you to watch hockey with me, India?" Gramps asks with a smug grin on his face.

"Yeah well, Jace wasn't playing before." And I can't help but wonder if this is the only game of his I'll have the chance to watch after today. "Do either of you want something to drink? I'm going to get a water."

"Give me Cohen," Gramps tells me, then lifts his arms and takes the baby from me. The old man smiles hesitantly at Cohen, and I stand, stuck in place, watching the two of them.

That little man has my heart, and I'm not sure teaching is my top priority anymore.

I move across the room to the private bar and order a bottle of water and another glass of pinot for Harper.

"Double-fisting it, Monroe?" Becket asks as he slides in next to me.

"The water is mine, Becks. The wine is for Harper." I nod her way and don't miss the way Beck's eyes widen when he sees my best friend. "You know, she's single."

"God, how we wish *he* was," Max says from beside me before ordering a drink. "Where's Kendall, Becket? I see she's not with us tonight."

"Don't say her name," Lenny teases, and Becks walks away, clearly not enjoying the teasing.

"Do you have a minute, Indy?" Max asks, and Lenny looks between us, unsure whether it's safe to leave us alone or not.

She makes her decision, takes a sip of the drink placed in

front of Max, and doesn't move. "Clearly, you're in need of a referee lately. Go on. I'm all ears."

"Low blow, Eleanor."

"Nice bruise, Maximus."

Lenny's husband comes over and wraps an arm around her shoulders. "Leave your brother alone, Len."

I watch the interaction, wondering if I can slip away unnoticed but deciding against it since I'm stuck in this box.

"I'm sorry if I make you uncomfortable, Indy. I just want to talk." Max sips the drink Lenny left on the bar, then turns back to watch the action on the ice. "I know my brother cares about you, and contrary to what he likes to think, I really do care about what's best for him."

"I'm not sure what you want me to do, Max. I honestly think this is something you and Jace have to work out between yourselves." My stomach somersaults with discomfort, standing here discussing this without Jace here feels wrong. Even worse than when Scarlet put me in this position weeks ago.

"I love my brother, Indy."

"I don't doubt that, Max. And deep down, I don't think Jace has ever doubted it either. I think he feels like you don't respect him, and you don't listen to him, and you don't treat him like a grown man living a good life. I also think talking to me instead of him is a mistake."

I turn away from him, ready to reclaim my safe spot between Gramps and Harper when Max's words stop me dead in my tracks. "I'm sorry. All I ever wanted was to keep our family together. We all splintered off into our own worlds in the years leading up to Dad's death. Lenny was in college in England, and Becks was in law school in Boston. I was in California, and we didn't even know Amelia existed."

"Stop." I put my hand up. "I'm not the one you owe these words to. He's out there on that ice, and I'm missing it, standing here talking to you. You've got two days of away games. Pick a day, find a time, and give those words to your brother. He deserves them. Not me. I'm no one."

"I hope you know how wrong you are, India. You're important to Jace, and that makes you one of us."

Yeah. Well, I guess we'll see how important I am now that I broke his heart.

# JACE

*I*t's the third period. We're down 4–3 with three minutes left on the clock when Boone passes me the puck. My adrenaline spikes as I skate down the ice and take the shot.

Everything happens double-time after that.

I'm cross-checked from behind and fly headfirst into the boards.

My stick leaves my hands, and my vision goes black.

The crowd roars as the ref comes to my side. "Did it go in? Did we score?"

"Don't move. You're medical team is coming."

"Did we get the goal?" I ask no one in particular when Doc Reese, the team's doctor, squats down in front of me.

"Yeah, Kingston. It counted. Now let's see how many guys I'm stitching up after the fight that just broke out." Doc helps me stand, then checks me out.

"I'm good," I tell him as the refs announce the penalties. A major for tripping, cross-checking, and boarding. The guy who got me is hit with five minutes in the box, and I'm given a penalty shot.

I skate over to O'Doul. "You okay to take the shot, Kingston?"

"Yeah, Coach. I'm good."

"Okay. This goalie is better with his body than his stick. Make him use the stick. Got me?"

"I got you, Coach."

I scored once in the first period, and my goal before the hit counts. So, we're tied 4–4.

If I get this, we're up by one.

It'd be nice if I wasn't seeing two of everything, but I don't tell Doc or Coach that.

I skate out to the other end of the ice and move the puck back and forth, waiting for the whistle to blow.

My eye catches on Indy standing with Cohen at the window of the family box.

She's here. She came.

The whistle blows, and I take off.

I gain momentum as I skate toward the goalie. Reading him, I deke left, forcing him to throw his body that way before shooting right.

Everyone in the arena holds their breath as the tinny sound of the puck hitting the post clinks before the puck glides in. The red light goes off, and the crowd loses their minds.

Hats are thrown on the ice. My teammates rush me in celebration before I'm pulled off for the next shift. The rink is cleared off, and the puck is placed back at center ice for the next face-off.

"Sit down, Kingston. You're done for the game. I want you to let Doc check you out in the locker room," O'Doul tells me in between shouts to Gagné.

"Not until we win this thing, Coach."

O'Doul grins, never taking his eyes off the ice. "That's what I figured."

It's the end of the period, and the shifts are running thirty seconds each between changes. The energy in the arena is a living, breathing thing as everyone counts down the last five seconds before the buzzer sounds and the game ends.

Five . . . Connor's got the puck.

Four . . . He passes to Boone.

Three . . . The Penguin's right wing is on Boone's ass.

Two . . . Is he going to shoot?

One . . . Time runs out and the Revolution wins.

And I just got my first hat trick in my very first professional game.

Ho-ly shit.

I turn and look up at the box, where my family is celebrating. And there they are. Indy and Cohen. Front and center, standing in the middle of the chaos. Damn.

As we filter into the locker room, Walker finds me and smacks my back. "Nice job out there, rookie."

O'Doul follows us, stopping in the middle of the room. "I'm gonna keep this short and sweet. You did good tonight. I saw the beginnings of a great team starting to gel out there. Nice win, men. Now you've got an hour before the buses pull out, and I'm opening the doors to the press in five minutes. Dinner is upstairs in the lounge. Do not miss the bus or you will not be playing in tomorrow's game."

He walks out, and I jump in the shower, hoping it'll clear my head.

By the time I'm getting dressed in front of my locker, the press has already descended like the plague.

Fuck, I hate the press.

A pretty woman in an expensive suit stops in front of my locker and smiles at me, then sticks her mic in my face. "Jace, how did it feel to play your first game for your brother's team? Do you think you made him proud?"

Walker steps into the shot in a towel barely covering his

shit and wraps an arm around me. "How about you ask Kingston how it feels to get his first hat trick in his first pro game? Or maybe ask him how he's feeling after getting cross-checked into the boards and then scoring on a penalty shot. Maybe don't go for the easy, lazy questions and don't ask him about his family."

He bends his knee and places one foot on the bench next to us, showing off everything he's got under that towel, and the attractive little reporter pretty much runs away.

"Thanks, man. I appreciate it." I don't bother telling him I'm shocked as shit that he just stuck up for me after all the shit he's given me the past few weeks.

"You're one of us now, Kingston, and we protect our own."

~

*T*hirty minutes later, the guys are going up to the conference room where dinner is set up. Everyone's trying to grab something to eat before we board the buses. They're going to take us to the plane that's flying us to Washington state for tomorrow's game.

I'm about to head up stairs to see my family when I walk out into the hall and see Indy leaning against the brick wall. She's wearing skintight blue jeans and my white away jersey, the number sixteen in bright red on the front.

*Goddamn, the things I'd like to do to this woman in that fucking jersey.*

A nervous smile pulls at her lips when she sees me. "Hey."

I look around to see where everyone else is. "Where's Cohen?"

"He's upstairs. Lenny offered to take him so I could wait for you down here." She lifts her eyes to mine, and I watch her chest rise and fall with each nervous breath. "I wanted a minute alone with you, Jace."

"Why? Seems like we said everything that needed to be said earlier."

"No." She reaches out with a hesitant hand and runs her thumb over the bruise under my eye. "I wanted to tell you I'm sorry, and I didn't want to do it over the phone. You deserve better than that, Jace."

"I deserve you, Indy. But only if you're in this with me. And I'm not so sure you are."

Her lips ghost over the bruise. "Don't give up on me yet, Jace. You asked me once to be patient with you. You said you didn't know what you were doing, and you were bound to screw up. Well, I don't know what I'm doing right now."

"The thing is, I don't just have myself to think about. I've got Cohen too. And you're thinking about leaving us. I don't know what to do about that," I tell her with as much honesty as I can. "Listen, I've got to get upstairs. I want to see Cohen before we leave."

"Okay," she agrees, seeming shaken. "Jace," she calls out as I walk away.

I stop and turn back to her, then catch her when she runs into my arms and presses her lips to mine. "I'll be here, ready to work this out with you when you get home."

"You sure about that?" I ask her, running my hand through her hair, not sure I'm ready to believe her yet.

"I might have been scared, Jace, but I wasn't ending us."

I stare into those beautiful golden eyes I love so damn much and want to believe her, but I can't do this here, and I can't fucking do it now.

"I've got to get up there now, Indy. I'll call you tomorrow before the walkthrough."

She nods and walks next to me until we step into my family's box. Everyone's here, excited for my first game and our first win. Lenny gives me a sleeping Cohen. It's way past my buddy's bedtime, and I fucking hate the idea I won't be able to see him for the next two days.

Max stays away from me, but I see him there, watching from the other side of the room.

In all the years I dreamed about playing my first professional game, this was never how I pictured it.

~

*A*lmost seven hours later, our plane is touching down in Seattle, and we're all exhausted. By the time we make it to the hotel and Quinn is passing out room keys, the whole team looks like the walking dead. Boone and I are bunked together, and the minute I walk into our room, I fall face-first on the bed and pass out.

I wake up the next morning to a text from Indy. It's a video of Cohen lying on the activity mat he loves so much. My baby is happy. His chubby legs are kicking in the air as he giggles, and my heart pangs in my chest. I hate that I'm missing this.

INDY

Good morning. By the time you get this, it'll probably be lunch time here in Kroydon Hills. I know you have a busy day, but I wanted to let you know Cohen and I miss you, and we'll be watching tonight.

JACE

Thanks. Give Cohen a kiss for me.

I'm not sure what else to say. But I don't get much of a chance to think about it before Boone lobs a pillow at my head. "Get your ass moving, man. I don't want to miss breakfast."

"Whatever, asshole." We shuffle into the conference room a few minutes later for a buffet breakfast laid out for the team, then get bussed over to the rink for our walkthrough. When we get back to the room, I try calling Indy, but she doesn't answer.

I hang up without leaving a voice mail.

Does anyone leave voice mails anymore?

Unlike yesterday, I don't have a problem taking a nap after today's walkthrough. My eyes grow heavy as soon as my head hits the pillow, and I fall asleep to thoughts of Indy and Cohen. Wondering where they are and what they're doing without me.

My alarm wakes me in time to jump in the shower, find Boone, and board the buses for our next game. We all go through our rituals again, but tonight O'Doul benches his starters in order to give some of the other guys a chance on the ice and him a better chance to evaluate everyone. I get some ice time but nothing like last night.

And when we get on the buses to head to the airport for tomorrow's game in Texas, I realize the day's over and I never talked to Indy. Only it's already after ten here, and they're three hours ahead of us.

Cohen's been sleeping pretty good lately, and I don't want to wake them up.

I'll call them tomorrow.

# INDIA

*W*ednesday morning, Cohen and I meet Harper for coffee at Sweet Temptations. Sophie and Amelia are working, but Soph said she'd sit with us for a few when the rush slows down. "Are you ready to talk about it yet?" Harper asks me as she stirs raw sugar into her Blue Mountain coffee.

"I don't know what to do, Harps. The fight was so nasty. I know I hurt him. And to be perfectly honest, I'm not even sure why I reacted the way I did. Jace was trying to be thoughtful, but all of a sudden, I just heard Atlas's voice in my head, reminding me I work for him. Yelling at me that Jace pays me and I sleep with him. And that as much as I wanted things to be easy, nothing worth having is ever easy, and I wouldn't even be in that house if I wasn't Cohen's nanny. We didn't move in together because he asked and I was so excited I couldn't say no. I moved in because it's part of my job, and the rest fell into place."

A throat clears, and I look up to find Amelia standing there with fresh chocolate croissants on a plate and a look of concern on her face.

*Great.*

"Mind if I give you some advice from a woman, who happens to be Jace's sister but was also in a similar situation years ago?"

"How much of that did you hear?" I adjust Cohen in his seat and push out the chair next to us for Amelia to sit.

She kisses Cohen's little hand and takes the seat. "I heard enough to know you're in a tough position. And I know Jace enough to guess how badly he responded to your fight."

"It gets worse." I tear off a piece of the warm, buttery croissant and pop it into my mouth, knowing even chocolate won't make this better. "After our big blowup, Kroydon Hills Prep called and offered me my dream job, and Jace heard the call."

"Oh, Indy, sweetie, you are screwed." Harper sips her coffee while she stares at the chocolatey goodness in front of her, trying hard to resist it.

"Just eat it, Harper. One won't kill you," I rip another piece off.

"You haven't seen my momma's hips. If I eat that, my dress for the event this weekend won't fit."

"Life without chocolate is a life wasted, Harper," Amelia argues before turning back to me. "I don't think you're screwed, Indy. I think a healthy dose of fear when you're falling in love is natural."

"Nobody said anything about love," I look down at the table, unable to meet Amelia's eyes.

"Oh, honey." Harper lays her hand over mine. "You keep telling yourself that."

Amelia quickly checks to make sure Sophie has the line under control. "Listen, I know not all of us like falling in love. It's scary, and it feels like there's no safety net to catch you at the bottom of the fall. But you've got to let go and trust that Jace will be there. He has the biggest heart out of all my brothers, and he loves you. I've seen it in the way he looks at you. I saw it that first night at the football game. It was like there was a tether holding him to you. He couldn't look away. Couldn't stay away. I didn't know Jace's mom before she died, but from what I'm told, she was amazing, and she gave Lenny and Jace a belief in love most of us don't have. At least, I know the rest of my siblings don't have it the same way those two do. Trust Jace. If you want to make this work, talk to him."

"I don't know, Amelia. He was so mad."

"So what? He'll either get over it or he won't. But you'll never know unless you try. Tell him how you feel. *But* . . . and this is a really big but. If your dream is to be a teacher, and you just got offered your dream job, you can't ignore it for my brother. We'll all help find another nanny for Cohen. But if teaching is what you want, it's what you need to do. You'll be a better wife and mother if you're fulfilled all by yourself, not dependent on them to fill you up. Trust me. I could be a stay-at-home mom if I wanted to. And some days, I wish I were, but I love this shop. I love every single little thing about it. I love knowing if, God forbid, something happened, I can take care of myself and my kids and Sam, if he'd let me. It's your call, but I wouldn't give that up. Not even for my husband."

I lift my gaze to Amelia's. "Do you hate me?"

"Absolutely not. Jace needs a strong woman. And one of the secrets to being a strong woman is knowing when to put yourself first and when to put your family first. It's a delicate balancing act. But once you figure it out, a really good life is waiting for you."

I rub my temple, trying to ignore the throbbing in my head. "Thank you, Amelia."

"Jace is a really good man who hides his feelings well, Indy. Don't let him hide them from you. And while you're at it, don't hurt him. Brothers aren't the only ones who get to be overprotective." She stands and pushes the chair in. "Now eat something, you're looking a little pale."

I don't bother telling her I'm pale from lack of sleep and not feeling great about the not-so-subtle threat she just threw my way.

Not that her threat should matter.

I have absolutely no intention of hurting Jace.

At least not more than I already have.

He's the one holding all the cards now.

~

I lay a blanket down in the backyard, so Cohen and I can enjoy the last vestiges of summer when my phone rings that afternoon. "Hold on," I say out loud as if my caller can magically hear me while I place Cohen on his tummy on the plush blanket. Once I pull the phone out and sit down next to my little man, his daddy's face flashes across my screen with an incoming FaceTime.

"Hi," I answer, so freaking happy to see his handsome face. "Give me a second."

I lie down next to Cohen and prop the phone up in front of us, so Jace can see us both and more importantly, so Cohen and I can both see him.

"I can't believe how much I missed you, little dude. I'll be home really late tonight, so I'll see you when you wake up in the morning. You be good for Indy." Obviously, Cohen doesn't respond to Jace, but for his daddy's sake, I wish he could.

"Congratulations on the win last night. I was bummed you didn't get to play. Are you feeling okay?"

Jace adjusts the phone, and my heart pulls with a longing so strong.

"Yeah, Coach wanted to evaluate some of the guys and rest some others. I'll be playing tonight though," he offers softly.

"Hey, Indy," Boone calls out from somewhere behind Jace.

I cringe. "I didn't realize you weren't alone."

"I was," Jace answers. "Boone's my babysitter. All the rookies have them. We're all rooming with vets, so they can show us the ropes." He turns his head away from me. "Knock it off, asshole."

I hear Boone laugh in the distance, then a door shutting.

"I've got a few minutes while he showers. How has Cohen been?"

"He's been a perfect little angel. We had coffee at Sweet Temptations today with Harper and your sister."

Jace furrows his brow. "Which sister?"

"Amelia." I don't add that she gave me advice on our relationship. "What time will you be home tonight?"

"It's about a four-hour flight, so I'm guessing I'll be at the house around four-ish. Have you looked into a new nanny?"

"Jace," I plead. "Can we just talk about all of this when you get home?"

"Fine. I'll see you tomorrow." He ends the call, and I hate myself a little more.

~

*J*ace

We won our game 5–4 and managed to get on the plane early, so it's a little before four by the time I get home the next morning. I'm exhausted and just want to hold my baby and my woman and deal with everything else tomorrow.

I let myself into the quiet house and make my way upstairs. Cohen is sleeping peacefully in his bassinet, and I swear to God, I think he grew two inches while I was gone. We're going to have to move him into his crib soon. Hopefully, this time he'll actually sleep in it.

I spend five minutes watching him sleep with my hand on his back, feeling him breathe. The selfish part of me wants to pick him up and have him sleep on my chest, but I don't. That's not fair to him, not to mention, with my luck, he'd wake up and want to party.

I don't think I can swing that right now.

Instead, I do the responsible thing and force myself to leave him, then walk into my room. I'm expecting Indy's sweet and spicy scent to hit me the second I walk through the door. What I'm *not* expecting is for her to be sleeping in my bed. It's like a sucker punch to the gut.

I asked her to share this room with me less than three days ago, and she flipped.

Now she's sleeping in here without me.

What the actual fuck?

She's got the blanket pulled up around her. Her golden hair is splayed out on one pillow and another is clutched in her arms like a security blanket.

Or like the way she likes to drape her arm over my chest.

I stand there, looking down at the golden goddess in my bed, debating what to do for a moment.

Eventually, I force myself back into Cohen's room. There's a day bed across from his bassinet that's the safer choice tonight, even if this thing isn't meant for guys over six feet tall.

~

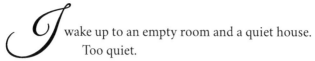 wake up to an empty room and a quiet house.
Too quiet.

*Shit.* What time is it?

I check my phone for the time and see a message from Indy.

INDY

I took Cohen for a walk around the lake. Be back around lunchtime.

Once I force myself out of bed, I jump in the shower and change, hoping to get some time with Cohen before I'm due at the rink. And maybe, if I'm being honest with myself, some time with Indy too. I know we need to talk, but I'm not sure I'm ready to hear what she has to say.

When I come downstairs, I'm expecting an empty house since it's still so quiet. Instead, I see Indy and Cohen tucked under a blanket in the crook of the couch. He's asleep on her chest, and her arm is wrapped around him. Eyes closed. Blonde lashes fanning her cheeks. But when I take a few steps closer, those lashes flutter, and her eyes open and raise to meet mine.

"Hi," she whispers, but there's something about the look on her face.

I stand in front of the two of them, hating this disconnect. "You okay?"

"Yeah. I just haven't slept great since you've been gone. I missed you."

I squat down in front of them and brush the soft hair out of her face, then gently press my lips against Cohen's head. "Me either." I lift him gently from her and hold him against me, needing to feel him. "I've never spent a night without him since the day he was born. Missing him for two entire days was hell."

"Yeah. I know the feeling." She sits up and tucks her feet under herself. "We need to talk, Jace."

"I know." I sit down on the couch and angle myself toward her. The pull to touch her is almost too painful to ignore. "Can you tell me what I did that was so wrong on Monday? I've been racking my brain for three days, trying to figure it out, and I've gotta tell you, I seriously have no fucking clue why you went off the way you did."

"Jace," She moves closer and leans against the back of the couch, not touching me but sending the hairs on my arm standing on end with even the slightest touch of her breath against my skin. "I got scared. All of a sudden, it just felt like we were ticking off boxes. I live here, *tick*. I take care of Cohen, *tick*. You and I are . . . whatever we are, *tick*. All of that happened, and it suddenly felt like I missed it actually happening. And then there you were, ready to move my stuff into your room. Ready to check off another box. Only none of that was you. It was me. I got scared and got stuck in my head, overanalyzing everything. It suddenly felt suffocating, and I'm not even sure why."

"Am I supposed to apologize for knowing what I want? Would it be better if I was some dick who strung you along or played some stupid fucking game? Because that's not me, Indy. It never has been. I know what I want, and I go for it."

She sits up on her knees and cups my face in her hands, the way I've done to her so many times before. "No. That wouldn't be better. I'm sorry, Jace. I didn't mean to hurt you. I got scared and freaked-out. I've never been in love before, and I needed a hot minute to process everything. Please say you can forgive me. Please tell me we can get past this."

"Say it again," I demand, needing to hear those words again.

"I got scared—"

"Not that."

Her golden eyes shimmer as a single tear drips down her cheek. "I love you, Jace Kingston. I'm not sure when it happened, but I'm sure this is real. I love you so much, it hurts to breathe when you're not around." Her thumb skims across my bottom lip. "You are mine. You and Cohen. You're my family. We've created this beautiful bubble I get to live in every day, and it's been the most natural thing I've ever done in my life." She scoots closer to me. "Don't you see? Falling in love with you was easy and fun. And you . . . you're larger than life. You're so sure of everything, and that scares me to death. Because I'm waiting for the other shoe to drop. In my life, it always does. I'm waiting for you to change your mind and not want me. I'm scared that I'm just convenient, and one day you'll wake up and realize you need more than convenient, and I don't know if I'd survive that."

"You were never convenient, pretty girl. You were always more. You were mine from the very first time I laid my eyes on you, and I think somewhere deep down we both knew it." I tug her toward me and bury my face in her hair. "You've got to talk to me about these things, Indy. I can't fix it if I don't know what's happening."

"If I promise I'll talk to you about everything . . . If I promise you I'll talk so much you'll get sick of me . . . Can you forgive me?"

"Have you made a decision about the teaching job?"

"No." She lays her head on my shoulder and closes her eyes. "I didn't want to make a decision until we talked about it. Together. If me freaking out the other day showed me anything, it was that we need to make decisions together."

The alarm goes off on my phone, and Cohen whines on my chest.

Shit.

I hand him back to Indy and silence the phone. "I'm sorry.

225

I've got to get to the rink for the walkthrough. Can we pick this up after the game?"

"Sure," she says, less than enthused, and I drop a kiss on her head.

"I'm sorry. I've got to go."

"See you tonight."

# INDIA

$\mathcal{E}$verything about tonight's game feels different.

Becks, Wren, and Sawyer are the only family in the box, other than Max and Daphne, so it's a much quieter night. Thankfully, that works wonders for my cranky pants, Cohen. Neither of us have been in the best mood this week. I think we both just missed his daddy.

And by the end of the third period, I think we're both ready for bed.

"You falling asleep over there, Indy?" Becket teases when he sees me yawn . . . again.

"No," I manage to answer unconvincingly, then laugh. "I'm just resting my eyes."

Wren leans across the table. "Are you feeling okay, Indie? You're not looking so good." She lifts her hand to my forehead, then pulls it away. "You're burning up."

"No." I stand up, then grip the table as the room spins around me. "I'm fine. Just tired."

"Hey now." Becks wraps an arm around my waist. "How about you sit back down?"

Wren looks from me to my grip on the table. "You're not

fine. I'm texting Jace to come up here after the game. You might be coming down with the flu."

"You're making a big deal out of nothing." I check to make sure Cohen is still asleep in his seat and then sit down and sip my water. Suddenly, I'm completely exhausted. And not loving the way the room spins. "Maybe you should call Jace."

~

*T*hought I only closed my eyes for a minute, but when I open them, Jace is pushing through the door. "Where is she?"

"Over here," I answer weakly.

He squats down in front of me and wraps his hand around the back of my neck. "Baby, what's going on?"

"Jace." It shouldn't be so difficult to push his name past my lips. "Something's wrong."

He takes my hands, pulling me to my feet, and I lean against his chest. "It's okay. Let's go home, pretty girl. I'll take care of you."

"Okay," I mutter before the world goes black.

~

*J*ace

"Indy, *baby*." I lift her in my arms and turn to Wren, helpless. "What happened?"

"Has she been sick, Jace?" She slides her fingers to the pulse point on Indy's wrist.

My fight-or-flight instinct kicks in. "I don't know. She hasn't said anything." I think about the way she looked this morning. *Shit.* I was in such a damn rush to get out of there, I missed it. I missed that she was sick. I should have realized something wasn't right. Then fear like I've never known before guts me. "Wren . . . she has a heart condition."

Max picks up Cohen's car seat and opens the door. "Let's go now, Jace. I'll drive."

And for the first time in months, I'm grateful for my brother.

We race down the hall and take the private elevator to Max's waiting car. I toss Becks my keys. "Cohen's car-seat base is in the SUV. Can you take him home?"

Daphne takes the keys from Becket's hand. "I've got Cohen, Becks. You go with them."

"Jace." Indy wraps an arm around my neck and lays her head against my chest. Her feverish skin burns through my shirt. "I don't feel good."

"Baby, you're gonna be fine. We're taking you to the hospital." I bury my face in her hair and whisper, "Please be okay. I love you, Indy. You've got to be okay."

My brothers help me get her into the car, and Wren slides in next to me with her phone in her hand. "Indy, honey. Who's your cardiologist? I'll call their service."

Indy mumbles something, then closes her eyes again.

"Do you know their name, Jace?" Wren pulls her phone out.

"Shit, Wren. I don't know." Jesus. I never asked her. I never asked her anything, once I found out she was okay.

She nods, then calls the hospital.

When we get to Kroydon Hills Hospital minutes later, Max pulls right up to the emergency room door and stops the car. A nurse with a wheelchair waits outside. "Ms. Monroe?" she asks as I help Indy out of the car and into the chair.

Wren rushes into action, filling the waiting nurse in on what happened as we all rush inside the building. The nurse disappears down a hall with my sister-in-law behind her, and I feel like my heart stops beating.

"Wren," I grab her hand before she's out of sight. "She has to be okay."

"I know, Jace. She's going to be fine." Then she's gone too, and I'm left standing in front of the closed door, helpless.

Max, Sawyer, and Becks force me into the empty waiting room we've seen the inside of too many damn times to count, and we wait.

This is the hospital my mother was in before we brought her home to die.

They brought my father here after the massive heart attack that killed him.

Wren came here after her car accident last winter.

I fucking hate this place.

My brothers and I sit in silence, watching the minutes tick by on an old clock hung above the door, each one slower than the last, until finally Sawyer's phone chimes with an incoming text. He pulls it out, then looks at me in concern. "She says they're still running tests, and it's going to be a while."

"Thanks," I mumble, trying to get a grip on my fear as everything slips further out of my grasp.

It takes nothing to feel like a man when everything is easy.

But when it's life and death . . . when you can't do a damn thing to fix it . . .

Well *then* you don't feel so tough.

Becks squeezes my shoulder. "How about Sawyer and I grab us some coffee?"

"Thanks." I rest my elbows on my knees and drop my head in my hands.

"You doing okay?" Max asks from the hard plastic chair a few seats down from me.

"No. I'm about to crawl out of my skin. I can't just sit here. I feel helpless." I lift my head and look at my oldest brother. "You ever feel helpless?"

"You're kidding, right?" Max moves so he's sitting next to me and mirrors my posture. "Yeah. I've felt helpless. Why do you think I'm such a fucking control freak?"

"Really? You seem like you've always got all the answers. Or at least like you *think* you've got all the answers." Okay, so maybe that was a low blow.

"Ouch." Max sits back. "I guess I deserved that. But honestly, put yourself in my shoes. I was twenty-five when Dad died, and I was thrust into the role of being the head of the family and the head of the business. Everyone had questions, and they all needed answers I didn't have. I had to learn how to control it all fast, and it's something I've clung to for nearly ten years."

He sits up and wipes his hands on his dress pants. "You know, I only ever tried to do what was right for the family. I guess that's why I drafted you. Don't get me wrong, you're still the best, and I always want the best, but I knew you didn't want to play for me. But I also knew we could lose you to any team anywhere in the country. If that happened, who knew if we'd ever get you back? If you went to play in California and loved it there, would you ever move home?"

He shakes his head, his voice strained. "We need you here, Jace. The whole family does. We're better when we're together, and I couldn't imagine you having a life the rest of us weren't part of. I know you fucking hate me for what I did, and you're right, it was selfish, but it was done out of love. Even if it wasn't what you wanted." He shrugs. "I guess maybe that means I was wrong."

We sit in silence while I try to process Max's *mea culpa,* and my head threatens to explode.

Then he quietly adds, "I'm sorry." And I think I might actually be hallucinating.

"Wait . . . what?" I must have heard him wrong. "Did you just admit you might be wrong about something?"

"Don't be a dick, Jace."

"Sorry. It's just I've been trying to explain this to you for months, and you haven't budged. Why the sudden change of heart?"

"Well, when your little brother clocks you in the middle of a team party, you take the time to reevaluate your choices. And when that doesn't work, you talk to his girlfriend, who hands you your ass and basically tells you to get your shit together. I run a multi-billion-dollar conglomerate, Jace. I've got my shit together, but I know I really fucked this up."

"She handed you your ass? When?"

Max laughs. "Monday night at the game. I made the mistake of asking her about you, and she basically told me to get off my ass and fix it. She's something special, Jace."

"Yeah. She is. She just got offered a job teaching at Kroydon Hills Prep." I realize how proud I am of her, and I didn't even bother to tell her. Just walked out instead. Fuck.

"Is she going to take it? It would be great to have someone at the school when the next generation takes it over in a few years."

"I don't know. We haven't talked about it." But I'm going to fix that as soon as I can. "I can't lose her."

"You won't." He wraps an arm around my shoulder and squeezes me the way Dad used to. "Every now and then, our family name can be a good thing. We'll get her whatever she needs. Whatever specialist. Christ, if we need to fly her to Zurich for an experimental procedure, we'll do it. I promise."

"Don't be so dramatic, Max." Wren runs her hand over my heavy head. I didn't even realize she'd walked up. "Indy's stable, Jace. She's going to be okay."

I stand up, desperate. "Can I see her?"

"I can take you back. But she's sleeping."

I turn to Max. "Could you and Daphne keep Cohen for me tonight?"

"Absolutely. Call me if you need anything."

"Thanks, brother." I grab him in a tight hug. "For everything, Max."

"Love you, Jace." He smacks my back. "Text later and let us know how she's doing."

"I will," I tell him, then follow Wren through the halls of Kroydon Hills Hospital until we get to the cardio wing.

"This is her room." Wren steps aside and lets me walk in first.

Indy's lying in a bed, hooked up to a monitor and IV. Her beautiful face is pale but relaxed while she sleeps. "Do they know what happened?"

"She has an infection. Unfortunately, they happen. They're giving her a strong round of IV antibiotics. I'd expect them to keep her for at least the next twenty-four hours."

I pull the seat in the corner of the room next to her bed and sit down, taking her hand in mine and pressing my lips against it. "Thank you, Wren. Thank you for everything. You keep making a habit of saving me."

"That's what big sisters are for." She kisses my cheek. "Did you call Carl yet?"

Shit.

"No. I didn't even think about it."

"Don't," Indy mumbles and weakly squeezes my hand.

"Baby, you're awake." I drop my head to our joined hands, desperate for the contact. "How are you feeling?"

"Don't call Gramps. It's late. He's already sleeping." She closes her eyes. "We'll deal with him tomorrow."

"Whatever you want, pretty girl."

Wren fills Indy's cup with ice water and adds a straw,

then pushes it in front of me. "I'm going to head home. I'll call the family and see who we can get to help you with Cohen over the next few days. Indy's not going to be in any shape to do it."

Indy's eyes fly open. "Who has him now?"

Wren shuts the door behind her as she leaves, and I lean over the bed and brush my lips over my girl's. "Daphne took him back to her house. Max is on his way back there now. He's fine."

"You need to go get him, Jace. He's going to be scared when he wakes up and neither of us is there." Tears fill her pretty eyes, and I swear to God, I'll do everything I can for the rest of my life to make sure she never cries again.

"He'll be okay for tonight. I'm not going anywhere. You scared the shit out of me, Indy. What happened?"

She licks her dry lips, so I pick up the cup of water and press the straw to her mouth. "Drink first. Talk second."

She rolls her eyes but sips like I tell her, so I'll count that as a win.

"I'm not sure. I've been so tired all week, but I thought it was because I slept like crap while you were gone. The fever came out of nowhere tonight. The doctor said I've got a nasty infection. They're going to keep me on IV antibiotics for at least twenty-four to forty-eight hours before they let me go home."

I run my thumb over her cheek, brushing away the tears.

"Don't cry, pretty girl. We've got this. I promise."

"Does that mean I didn't push you away?" Her lower lip trembles, and I lose any semblance of self-control.

I lower the railing on the side of the bed and slide in next to her, careful not to move her much, then pull her against me. "I love you, India Monroe. You're not getting rid of me. Plus, I heard you knocked some sense into Max. You're going to have to teach me your trick. I've been trying to do that for years."

She lays her head on my chest and sniffles. "I was so scared I broke us, Jace. All I kept thinking was I broke us before we ever really had a chance."

"We're not broken, Indy, and I don't scare that easily. We've got a lifetime ahead of us, and it's going to be such an incredible life."

# INDIA

"*J*ace . . . You know I can walk, right?" From the minute he wheeled me out of the hospital, this man has refused to let my feet touch the ground.

Incredibly sweet? Yes.

Practical? Not at all.

"I know. It doesn't mean I'm letting you go just yet though." He carries me through the garage and into the house, then finally sets me down on the couch. "Let me get you a blanket."

"Stop." I grab his hand. "I'm not cold. I'm just glad to be home. I was worried they were going to try to keep me another night. Two days was two days too long. Now, where's Cohen?"

"He's right here," Becks announces as he walks into the room, looking less than rested. "He's slept. He's eaten. And he's destroyed two diapers. Seriously, maybe you should consider changing what you feed this kid. That can't be natural. I mean, how can so much shit come out of such a small body?"

"Thank you, Becket." I reach out my arms and smile wildly when he gives me Cohen. I kiss his perfect little face and breathe in my sweet boy who I missed, like a part of myself had been ripped away.

"Happy to help. But I need you to do me a favor now, Indy," Becks answers with a sly wink.

"Leave her alone, Becket. We just got home," Jace fires back, fully prepared to take hovering to new levels.

"I was just going to say, we need her to stay healthy and out of the hospital. I don't make a very good babysitter, brother." He grins, then claps his hands together. "And on that thought, I'm going to leave the three of you alone. I left those papers you asked for on the kitchen counter."

"I'll be right back. I'm just going to walk Becks out."

I ignore Jace and nuzzle Cohen's neck. "I missed you so much, little man."

He sucks his binky with wide eyes staring back up at me, and I'm pretty sure I'll never be able to put him down again. Forget leaving him to teach. I don't know if I can do it.

Jace walks back in a few minutes later with my laptop under one arm and a folder under another. He sets them both down, then grabs my feet and pulls them into his lap. "We've got to talk, pretty girl."

"Do we have to? I just want to enjoy being here with both of you before you have to get to the arena for tonight's game." I lay my head on his shoulder and close my eyes.

Okay, so maybe that was a little whiney, but I think I should get a pass after two days in the hospital.

"Sorry. We've got to clear a few things up before I leave." He presses a featherlight kiss against my forehead, then picks up the manilla folder and pulls out a white legal document. "This is your contract."

Then he rips it in half and tosses it on the table.

"Jace," I gasp.

"No, Indy. The only thing you were right about this week was that you work for me."

"Hey." I try to act outraged, but it doesn't work. "Fine. You're right. I was wrong about everything else. But what does that have to do with you tearing my contract in half?"

"You're officially fired." Jace's smile is beautiful as he pulls a velvet box from his pocket, and I think I'm about to hyperventilate.

"Jace . . ." Oh God.

He slides off the couch and onto one knee, then holds up the little black box. "I love you, India Monroe. Will you move in with us, not because you work for me but instead because you love Cohen and me?" He cracks open the box, and a shiny new house key sits nestled on the pillow. "Just for clarification, I want you in my house and in my bed every night and every morning. I want your dirty clothes mixed with mine. I want you to help me find a new nanny to watch Cohen during the day because you'll be busy teaching the next generation at Kroydon Hills Prep. I want you, Indy. Not because you work for me. But because you love me."

"Really?" My heart somersaults inside my chest. "You want me to take the job? I don't even know if it's still available. I haven't answered them yet."

"Let's just say a little birdie told me it's still available."

I reach forward and take the box with shaking hands. "But how . . . ?"

"Max sits on the board of trustees. He had no idea they were offering *you* the job, but he made a call for me yesterday to see if it was still available, and it is. It's your dream job, Indy. You've got to take it."

Once Jace sits back on the couch, I move onto his lap and cuddle Cohen between us. "It may be my dream job, Jace. But you and Cohen are my dream. Are you sure this is what you want?"

"Yeah, pretty girl. I want you to take it."

With a shaky breath, I nod. "Okay."

"Yeah? Does this mean I can move your stuff into my room without you freaking out?"

I narrow my glare. "Never going to let me live that down, are you?"

"Nope," Jace laughs, then kisses me. "Never. I'm going to torture you about it until we're old and gray. Then I'm going to sit out back on a rocking chair, watching the falls hit the lake, and tell our grandchildren about that time their grandmother overreacted. I'll use it as a scare tactic when they want to do something stupid, like jump off the waterfalls."

I suck in a breath. He paints such a vivid picture, I can see it clearly. "Promise?"

"Oh yeah. You and me, pretty girl. We're going to live a great life."

"I love you, Jace." I skim my lips along his jaw. "I think I always have."

"I love you too, Indy. And I know I always will."

# EPILOGUE

## INDIA

*One year later – Thanksgiving*

The tell-tale sound of Cohen ready to get out of his crib wakes me up early Thanksgiving morning. My little man likes to shake the bars of his crib, like an inmate demanding release from his cell. Dramatic to the end, just like his father.

I push back the covers, but Jace wraps his arms around me and presses his lips against my head. "Go back to sleep, pretty girl. I've got him."

His lips skim down my neck and over my shoulder, making it hard for me to form words. "Hmm . . . Are you sure?"

He drags a hand under my nightgown and up my warm skin, and I practically melt in response. I roll over and reach a hand down his boxers and enjoy the hiss that leaves his lips. My mouth skims along his jaw as I slide my thumb over the tip of his crown. "Can you be quick?"

"Can you be quiet?" he counters.

I shove his boxers down and roll on top of him, straddling his hips, then lift up and slowly sink down over his hard

241

length. And just like the first time, the air wooshes from my lungs.

"You're so tight, baby." Jace jackknifes up and cups my ass in his hands, controlling me, even when I'm on top, and I let him. Because damn, this man. He knows every inch of my body and exactly what I need. Especially when we need to make it fast.

I rock against him, pressing my lips to his, and we swallow each other's moans.

"I'm close, Jace," I whisper.

His hands move under my night gown and dig into my soft flesh as he captures one breast in his mouth, sucking and teasing and biting my nipples until I'm ready to scream. "Somebody woke up needy this morning."

He slides his tongue inside my mouth and even now, a year later, I get lost in his kiss. But Jace has other ideas. He thrusts up and pushes a finger inside my ass, and a kaleidoscope of color explodes behind my eyes. Every vibrant shade of the rainbow bursts before me as my climax rocks me to my core. Wave after wave of warmth pulls me under until I can't even hold my head up and instead, drop it to Jace's shoulder, unable to move.

I lay my limp body against his, my arms circled around his neck and my nightgown shoved up between us as we sit in silence. Neither of us able to move yet. "I love our mornings."

"Momma . . ."

Oh no.

Both our heads turn in slow motion when the little voice calls my name. Because the little voice is no longer in his room. Nope. Cohen stands in our open bedroom door, his favorite blanket squished in his fist. And I'm sitting on the bed with his father's still semi-hard dick between my legs and his come leaking down my thighs.

Oh shit.

"I told you it was time to lower the mattress again," I force out between gritted teeth.

"Move your nightgown to cover me so I can pull up my boxers," Jace mumbles through a less than sane smile.

Once he's tucked back into his boxers, I move off Jace's lap and ignore the wet spot on the sheets. "Come here, honey. Do you want pancakes for breakfast?"

Cohen climbs up onto our bed, then plops down right between Jace and me. His dark-brown hair stands up in every direction, and those navy-blue eyes of his glitter with happiness. Our boy wakes up every day happy and smiling. Ready for his day. But when I lean over to kiss his cheek, I notice his pajamas aren't the ones I changed him into after his bath last night.

Mickey Mouse has been replaced.

I look closer and realize he's still wearing his favorite footies, but now they're covered by a white t-shirt with black writing. "What are you wearing?"

I tug the shirt down so I can read what it says, then make him stand up on the bed to make sure I'm not hallucinating.

*Will you marry my daddy?* is written in black stitching across the shirt.

When my eyes fly to Jace's, he's holding a curled-up piece of paper with a gold ribbon wrapped around it, and a diamond ring is nestled in the center of the bow.

"Jace . . ."

He picks up Cohen and places him in his lap.

Thankfully, the blanket is between Cohen and him.

*We've got to get a lock on that door.*

"I'd planned to make you breakfast in bed, then surprise you when Cohen and I came into the room. But I guess neither of your Kingston men are good at waiting. We know what we want, Indy. And we want you."

"You've got me, Jace." I roll my trembling lips together, trying to hold back the happy tears threatening to break free. "You've both had me since the first day I walked through that door."

Jace unties a stunning cushion-cut diamond ring and slips it on my finger. "Marry me, Indy. I love you more than I ever knew I could love anyone. Let me spend the rest of my life loving you and our family. Be my wife."

I nod frantically. "Yes, Jace. I'll be your wife."

He gathers my face in his hands and brushes a kiss over my lips.

So many times, this man has taken my breath away, but today, his kiss breathes life into me. Holding a promise I know he'll never break.

Cohen jumps up, wanting to join in on the hug, and Jace pulls back and gives him the roll of paper. "Give this to Momma, buddy."

Cohen started calling me *Momma* a few weeks ago. He'd been saying *Daddy* for months, but he never called me *Mommy* or *Momma* when we were talking about me. He just decided one night at a football game that, that was my name and I may have cried the first time. Okay, and maybe the next time too. In reality, I've cried for the past few weeks. I wasn't sure what to think of it. But I haven't been his nanny in over a year. We were lucky enough to find Mrs. Bennet pretty quickly, once we started looking last year. Cohen loves her, and thankfully, so do we. She's great with him, and bonus, she loves to cook too. We didn't see a need for her to move in since I was only working until three every day, which was exactly what she was looking for.

My mom used to say everything happens for a reason.

If you're lucky, you might eventually be able to see what that reason is, but most of us just have to have faith. My two months spent as Cohen's nanny were the most important two months of my life.

They gave me Jace and Cohen.

They helped me believe in myself enough to find my dream job.

They reminded me that family is a pain in the ass, but they're also *everything*.

Cohen hands me the rolled-up tube of paper by smacking me with it, and I pull him down into my lap. "What's this, baby? Will you help me untie it?"

With my hand over his, we tug at the gold ribbon until it falls free from the paper, then unroll it.

## PETITION FOR ADOPTION

"Jace . . ." I scan down the rest of the document and don't even realize I'm crying until Jace wipes the tears from my face. "I don't know what to say."

"You're already his mother, Indy. I thought it was about time we made it official."

"I love you, Jace Kingston." I fight a losing battle to stop crying but give up and put the paper down. "I guess I have something for you too."

"You've got a present for me?" Jace asks with the same excitement Cohen has when I put ice cream in front of him.

"I guess you could call it that." I lean over and open my nightstand drawer, taking out the blue gift bag and handing it to him. "Go ahead. It's actually for both of you."

Jace makes a funny face, then let's Cohen rip the blue and white tissue paper out of the bag before he pulls out the matching navy-blue t-shirts. He looks at his shirt that says *Daddy* across the front, then unfolds Cohen's shirt and holds it up to our son, who's over this morning's shenanigans already and is trying to sneak off the bed.

*Big Brother* is printed in block lettering on the front of Cohen's shirt, and now it's Jace's turn to look shocked. "You're pregnant?"

"Are you angry?"

"Are you kidding? No, baby. I'm not angry. When did you find out?"

"Yesterday. I realized I was a few weeks late when I looked at the calendar Monday. So I made an appointment with Wren. Turns out, we're having another baby, and we may never have sex again in October," I tease.

"What?" The poor man looks incredibly confused.

"Baby Kingston number two is due three days before Cohen's birthday." Leave it to Jace to have superhuman sperm that even the shot can't stop.

"I guess we've got a whole lot to be thankful for this year."

I grab Cohen before he can make his getaway, then hug my two favorite guys.

"We sure do."

~

**Jace**

I'm sitting on the couch with Atlas, watching football, when Indy comes downstairs with Cohen that afternoon. "He's got a turkey on his butt."

Indy giggles and shakes Cohen's chubby butt in my face. "You bet your sweet ass he does."

I stand and take Cohen from her as she plants a fat kiss on my lips. "Give me five minutes, and I'll be ready to go." Her ring glints in the sunlight, and I think about all the ways I'm going to fuck my fiancé with nothing but that ring on later tonight.

"Hurry up. I'm hungry," Atlas grumbles from the couch.

She rests her forehead against my chest. "Remind me again why we had to invite him to Thanksgiving dinner?"

I grip the back of her neck and angle her head up. "Because your grandfather is having dinner with Gladys, and you didn't want your brother to be alone."

"Yeah, sis," the moron agrees. "Listen to hockey boy and be nice to me. I've got a game tomorrow night. I need sustenance. Let's go."

"I'm surprised he knows what the word *sustenance* means." Indy scowls.

"You're not the only one with a fancy degree, India," Atlas responds in annoyance. He watches his sister storm up the stairs and laughs. "Are you sure you want to marry her?"

"You'll get it one day." I grin smugly, thinking about how we woke up this morning and consider torturing him with a few details.

"Whatever you say, hockey boy."

I should have fallen in love with an only child.

Or maybe I should have *been* an only child.

Max stands and lifts his wine glass into the air. "I'd like to thank you all for coming today. It's the first time we've sat around a table instead of being at a stadium on Thanksgiving in a few years, and I can't help but remember all the times we did this growing up. We look a little different now than we did then. A little older. Hopefully, a little wiser. And we've added a few more faces . . ."

Becks fakes a cough. "Condoms, people. You all need to buy stock in condoms."

Lenny glares. "Language, Becket."

Becks laughs and sips his wine. "It's not like I said S-E-X, Eleanor."

Ashlynn flicks Becket's ear. "Your little sister can spell, Becket."

Max clears his throat, unsuccessfully trying to get everyone's attention.

He'd have better luck trying to herd cats.

"Give it up, Maximus." Hudson taps his wine glass to our oldest brother's. "I'm thankful for everyone at this table, and I think Max is too. Now, let's eat."

"Not yet," Daphne cuts Hudson off. "I thought we could go around the table and each say something we're grateful for."

"Oh come on, Pollyanna. Seriously?" Scarlet laughs. "We're all thankful for each other and this food."

I lean down and brush my lips over Indy's ear. "You sure you want to join my crazy family, pretty girl?"

"What?" Amelia gasps. "Is there something you're not telling us, Jace?"

Indy blushes furiously, then holds up her ring finger for everyone to see.

"She said *yes*," I announce to the room.

"Congratulations, brother." Sawyer pounds my shoulder.

Wren jumps up to hug us both. "Do you guys have a date set yet?"

"No." Indy links her hand in mine. "He just asked this morning, so we haven't had time to talk about it."

"I was actually thinking we could do it on Christmas Eve. You know, since the league gives us off Christmas Eve, Christmas Day, and the day after." Judging by the look on Indy's face, she's not thrilled with the idea.

"Christmas Eve of *this* year? As in one-month-from-now Christmas Eve?" Her eyes grow wide with concern.

"That's what I was thinking."

"Jace Kingston, are you insane?" I'm fairly sure Scarlet's asking a rhetorical question, but judging by the way she's looking at me right now, I think she might actually want an answer.

"No?" I try to sound convincing, but it definitely comes out more question than statement.

"Why are men so clueless?" Scarlet asks, and I'm not touching this one with a ten-foot pole. "Indy, why don't we get together tomorrow? I'll help you with the planning since my boneheaded brother thinks getting this done in a month will be easy."

"Oh." Amelia perks up. "Why don't you meet at Sweet Temptations, and I can help you?"

"Good idea," Lenny adds. "I'll help too."

"Not without me," Wren tells the girls, and Daphne and Maddie agree.

All the while, Indy's grip on my hand tightens. "You really want to try to pull this together in a month?"

"Pretty girl, I'd marry you tomorrow if we could. I'm barely willing to wait a month."

Hudson moves Indy's wine glass away from her place setting, and she furrows her brow. "What are you doing?"

"I just figured wine wasn't good for you if . . . you know," Hud backtracks sheepishly.

"It's not wine you idiot." She grabs the glass back. "It's water."

"Wait . . . Does that mean . . . ?" Lenny bounces in her seat.

Wren blows out a breath. "Oh thank God. I suck at keeping secrets."

"You knew?" Sawyer asks, shocked.

"Of course I knew. This family alone could keep me in business with all the babies and pregnancies."

I kiss Indy's cheek. "I love you, baby."

My girl looks at me like she's deciding between love and murder.

"I guess it's going to be a crazy four weeks."

# The End . . . for now.

# WHAT'S NEXT?

Ready for the next books in The Defiant Kings Series?

Preorder Becket Kingston's story in Overruled: https://bit.ly/OverruledDefiantKings4

# ACKNOWLEDGMENTS

M. ~ You are everything. Thank you for holding my hand and wiping my tears. Thank you for loving me and showing our sons what true love looks like.

My dream team, Brianna and Heather ~ I will never be able to thank you enough for everything you have done for me. There are no words that feel big enough.

Dena ~ Without you, I would have never made this deadline and I will be forever grateful for your support, long voice memos and insane attention to detail.

Sarah ~ I will follow you anywhere.

Shannon ~ This cover is everything. Thank you for making Jace perfect.

Vicki, Jen & Kelly ~ I am so lucky to have you in my corner and to count you as my friends.

For all of my Jersey Girls ~ Thank you for giving me a safe space and showing me so much grace over the last few months.

To all of the Indie authors out there who have helped me

along the way – you are amazing! This community is so incredibly supportive, and I am so lucky to be a part of it!

Thank you to all of the bloggers who took the time to read, review, and promote Iced. I promise to get the next book to you earlier!

And finally, the biggest thank you to you, the reader. I hope you enjoyed reading Jace and Indy as much as I loved being lost in their world.

# ABOUT THE AUTHOR

Bella Matthews is a Jersey girl at heart. She is married to her very own Alpha Male and raising three little ones. You can typically find her running from one sporting event to another. When she is home, she is usually hiding in her home office with the only other female in her house, her rescue dog Tinker Bell by her side. She likes to write swoon-worthy heroes and sassy, smart heroines with a healthy dose of laughter thrown in.

**Stay Connected**

Amazon Author Page: https://amzn.to/2UWU7Xs

Facebook Page: https://www.facebook.com/bella.matthews.3511

Reader Group: https://www.facebook.com/groups/599671387345008/

Instagram: https://www.instagram.com/bella.matthews.author/

Bookbub: https://www.bookbub.com/authors/bella-matthews

Goodreads: https://www.goodreads.com/.../show/20795160.Bella_Matthews

TikTok: https://vm.tiktok.com/ZMdfNfbQD/

Newsletter: https://bit.ly/BMNLsingups

Patreon: https://www.patreon.com/BellaMatthews

## ALSO BY BELLA MATTHEWS

### Kings of Kroydon Hills

All In

More Than A Game

Always Earned, Never Given

Under Pressure

### Restless Kings

Rise of the King

Broken King

Fallen King

### The Risks We Take Duet

Worth The Risk

Worth The Fight

### Defiant Kings

Caged

Shaken

Iced

Overruled (Coming soon)

# CHECK OUT BELLA'S WEBSITE

Scan the QR code or go to http://authorbellamatthews.com
to stay up to date with all things Bella Matthews

Made in United States
Orlando, FL
31 January 2025